Uwe Timm

The Invention of Curried Sausage

Translated by Leila Vennewitz

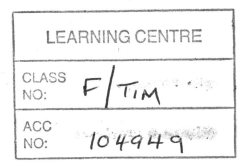

A NEW DIRECTIONS BOOK

Manufactured in the United States of America.
New Directions Books are printed on acid-free paper.
First published in 1993 as *Die Entdeckung der Currywurst*
by Kiepenheuer & Witsch, Cologne.
First published clothbound by New Directions in 1995.
Published simultaneously in Canada by Penguin Books Canada
Limited.

Library of Congress Cataloging-in-Publication Data
Timm, Uwe, 1940–
[Entdeckung der Currywurst. English]
The invention of curried sausage/Uwe Timm; translated by
Leila Vennewitz.
p.   cm.
ISBN 978-0-8112-1368-4
I. Vennewitz, Leila.   II. Title.
PT2682.I39E5813   1995
833'.914—dc20   94-41982   CIP

New Directions Books are published for James Laughlin
by New Directions Publishing Corporation
80 Eighth Avenue, New York 10011
SEVENTH PRINTING

The Invention
of Curried Sausage

The Invention
of Curried Sausage

for Hans Timm (1899–1958)

1

IT'S BEEN A GOOD TWELVE YEARS
since I ate my last curried sausage at Mrs. Brücker's
stand. The food stand was on Grossneumarkt, a
square in the harbor district: windy, dirty, and paved
with cobblestones. There are a few scrubby trees on
the square, a public toilet, and three stands where
high-school kids meet and drink Algerian red wine
served from plastic containers. To the west, gray-
green, the glass façade of an insurance company, and
beyond that St. Michael's church, whose spire casts a
shadow on the square in the afternoon. During the
war that part of the city had been virtually destroyed
by bombs. Only a few streets were spared, and on one
of them, Brüderstrasse, an aunt of mine used to live.
I often visited her as a child, although secretly, my
father having forbidden me to go there. The area was
known as Little Moscow, and the red-light district
was not far off.

Later, whenever I visited Hamburg I used to go to
that district and walk through the streets, past the
building where my aunt, who had been dead for years,
once lived, so that finally—and this was the real

reason—I could go to Mrs. Brücker's food stand and eat her curried sausage.

"Hello there!" said Mrs. Brücker, as if she'd seen me only the day before. "Same as usual?"

She was busying herself with a large cast-iron frying pan. Now and again a gust would blow drizzle under the narrow awning: an army tarpaulin, mottled gray and green, but so full of holes that it had been covered with an extra sheet of plastic.

"Nothing doing here anymore," said Mrs. Brücker as she lifted the sieve of french fries out of the bubbling oil, and she would tell me about all the people who had meanwhile died or moved away from the area. Names that meant nothing to me had had strokes, shingles, late-onset diabetes, or were now lying in Ohlsdorf cemetery. Mrs. Brücker still lived in the same building as my aunt once had.

"There!" She held out her hands to me, slowly turning them over. The knuckles were gnarled. "It's gout. My eyes aren't what they used to be either. Next year," she said, as she did every year, "I'm going to give up the stand, for good." With wooden tongs she fished one of her pickled cucumbers out of the jar. "You used to like these even as a youngster." She had never charged me for the pickle. "How in the world can you stand living in Munich?"

"They have food stands there too."

That's what she'd been waiting for because then—this was part of our ritual—she would say: "Ye-es, but do they have curried sausage too?"

"No, at least not as good."

"You see?" she said, sprinkling some curry powder into the hot pan. Then with a knife she sliced some veal sausage into it, adding *"Weisswurst,* horrible, and then sweet mustard! It's enough to turn your stomach, isn't it?" She gave herself an exaggerated shudder. "Brr," then plopped some ketchup into the pan, stirred, shook a bit more black pepper over it, and finally pushed the sausage slices onto the crimped paper plate. "This is the genuine article. Has something to do with the wind. Believe me. With a cold wind you need hot stuff."

Her stand really was set up on a windy corner. The plastic sheet was torn where it was fastened to the stand, and now and again a strong gust would tip over one of the large plastic cone-shaped tables, advertising ice cream, at which you could stand as you ate your meatballs and, of course, that absolutely unique curried sausage.

"I'm going to close the stand, for good."

She said this every time, yet I was sure I would see her again the following year. But the following year her stand had disappeared.

As a result I stopped going back to that area,

scarcely ever thought of Mrs. Brücker, except occasionally at a food stand in Berlin, Kassel, or somewhere, and then, of course, whenever connoisseurs began arguing about the place and date of origin of curried sausage. Most of them—almost all of them, in fact—claimed it had been the Berlin of the late fifties. At that point I would always bring Hamburg, Mrs. Brücker, and an earlier date into the conversation.

Most of them doubted that curried sausage had been invented. Or by anyone in particular for that matter. Little myths, fairy tales, sagas, legends—told and retold. Is there one inventor of meatballs? Isn't such food a collective achievement? Food slowly created out of the logic of prevailing conditions, as may have happened with meatballs, for instance: People had left-over bread and just a little meat but wanted to fill their stomachs, so the obvious thing to do was to take both and then enthusiastically mash them together. Many will have done this, in various places—witness the different regional names for meatballs.

"Possibly," I would say, "but with curried sausage it's different, the name's enough to tell you that. It combines the farthest with the nearest, curry with sausage. And that combination, which amounted to an invention, goes back to Mrs. Brücker and dates from sometime in the mid-forties."

This is what I remember: I am sitting in my aunt's

kitchen on Brüderstrasse, and in this dark kitchen with its painted ivory-colored walls, Mrs. Brücker, who lives on the topmost floor in the attic, is also sitting. She is telling us about the black-market dealers, longshoremen, sailors, small- and big-time crooks, the hookers and pimps who come to her stand. Hard to believe what went on! All for real. Mrs. Brücker maintained that it was because of her curried sausage: it loosened the tongue, sharpened the eye.

That's what I remembered and began to investigate. I asked relatives and friends. Mrs. Brücker? Some could remember her quite well. And the food stand, too. But had she invented curried sausage? And how? No one could tell me that.

Even my mother, who remembered all kinds of things down to the smallest detail, knew nothing about the invention of curried sausage. Acorn coffee—now that Mrs. Brücker had experimented with over a long time, since in those days people had next to nothing. Acorn coffee was what she served when she opened her food stand after the war. My mother could even still tell me the recipe: Gather some acorns, dry them in the oven, remove the cups, then, after grinding and roasting the kernels, add the usual ersatz coffee blend. The coffee tasted a little bitter. Anyone who drank that coffee for a long time, so my mother claimed, gradually lost their sense of taste. Acorn coffee actually tanned the tongue, so that, during the starvation winter of 1947, acorn-coffee drinkers could even bake sawdust into their bread and think it tasted as good as bread made from the finest wheat flour.

And then there was also the story about her husband. "Mrs. Brücker was married?" "Yes. She kicked him out one day."

"Why?"

My mother couldn't tell me that.

So one morning I went to Brüderstrasse. The building had been renovated. Mrs. Brücker's name was, as I expected, no longer on the bell board. The worn wooden stairs had been replaced by new ones edged with brass strips. The automatic light in the stairwell was bright and gave me enough time to climb to the top: in the old days it had stayed on for only thirty-six stairs. As kids we used to race the light all the way up the stairs to the top floor, where Mrs. Brücker lived.

I walked through the streets of the district, narrow treeless streets. This was where longshoremen and shipyard workers used to live. Now the buildings had been renovated and the apartments—the downtown area is not far off—turned into luxury premises. In place of dairy, grocery, and drygoods stores, now there were boutiques, beauty parlors, and art galleries.

Only Mr. Zwerg's little stationery shop was still there. In the narrow display window, among dusty cigar and cigarillo cases, stood a man wearing a topee and holding a long pipe.

I asked Mr. Zwerg whether Mrs. Brücker was still alive and, if so, where she might be living.

"What are you after?" he asked, tense with suspicion. "The shop's already been rented."

As proof that I knew him from the old days, I told him how once—it must have been in 1948—he had climbed a tree, the only tree in the area that hadn't burned down in the nightly air raids or later, after the war, been chopped up for firewood. An elm tree. A cat being chased by a dog had fled up it and climbed higher and higher until it couldn't climb down again. It spent the whole night in the tree, as well as the next morning. Thereupon Mr. Zwerg, who had served with the combat engineers, had climbed up after the animal under the eyes of many curious onlookers. But the cat had escaped higher and higher into the treetop, and suddenly Mr. Zwerg too was high up in the tree and unable to get down again. The fire engine had to come and, using a ladder, brought both Mr. Zwerg and the cat down out of the tree. After listening silently to my story, Mr. Zwerg turned away, took out his left eye, and polished it with a handkerchief. "Those were the days," he said. He put back his eye and blew his nose. "Yes," he said at last, "I was surprised to find myself so high—from up there I couldn't judge the distance properly."

He was the last of the former inhabitants of the building. Two months earlier the new landlord had notified him of a rent increase, one which it was impossible to pay. "Otherwise I'd have carried on, though I'll be eighty next year. You get to see people that way. Pension? Sure. Enough so you won't starve, but you can't live on it either. A wine bar's coming in here now. I thought at first it was some kind of music business. Mrs. Brücker? No, she left long ago. She must be dead by now."

But then I did meet her again after all. She was sitting by the window, knitting. Subdued sunlight entered through the blinds. There was a smell of oil, floor wax, and old age. Downstairs near the reception desk, a number of old women and a few old men were sitting right and left along the walls of the corridor, most of them wearing felt slippers and many with braces on their hands, staring at me as if they had been waiting for days for my arrival. 243 was the room number given me at the desk. I had been to the citizens' registry where they had told me her address, a municipal old-age home in Harburg.

I didn't recognize her. Her hair had already been gray when I last saw her; now it had become thin, her nose seemed to have grown larger, her chin too. The once bright blue of her eyes had turned milky. However, her knuckles were no longer swollen.

She claimed to remember me distinctly. "Came to see me as a boy, didn't you, and sat with Hilde in the kitchen. Later on you sometimes used to come to the food stand." And then she asked if she might touch my face. She put aside her knitting. I felt her hands, a fleeting, groping search. Delicate, soft palms. "The gout has gone, but instead I can't see anything. So there is something like divine compensation. You don't have a moustache anymore, and your hair's not so long now." She looked up and in my direction, but still slightly beyond me, as if someone were standing there. "The other day a man was here," she said, "trying to palm off a magazine on me. I don't buy a thing."

As soon as I spoke she adjusted her gaze and now and then looked me in the eye. I just wanted to ask her something: Was I right in remembering that shortly after the war she had invented curried sausage?

"Curried sausage? No!" she said. "I just had a food stand!"

For a moment I thought it would have been better not to have come and asked her at all. Then I would have gone on having a story in my head that did indeed combine a flavor and my childhood. Now, after this visit, I might just as well make up anything I liked.

She laughed, as if she could see my perplexity, my disappointment even, which I had no need to hide.

"It's true," she said, "but nobody here will believe me. They just laughed when I told them about it. Said I was nuts. These days I don't go downstairs much anymore. Yes," she said, "I invented curried sausage."

"How?"

"It's a long story," she replied. "You'll need to have some time to spare."

"I have."

"Maybe when you come again," she said, "you can bring along a slice of cake. And I'll make us some coffee."

Seven times I made the trip to Harburg, seven afternoons the smell of floor wax, Lysol, and old cooking fat, seven times I helped her shorten the afternoons that slowly faded to evening. She called me by my first name. Out of habit, I called her Mrs. Brücker.

"There's nothing more to expect, and then you lose your eyesight." Seven times cake, seven times massive, rich, sweet wedges: Prince Regent, Sacher, mandarin cream, cheese cake with whipped cream; seven times Hugo, a friendly conscientious objector who was doing his alternate service, brought her pink blood-pressure pills, seven times I exercised patience, watched her knit, the needles clicking swiftly and evenly. The front of a sweater for her great-grandson was taking shape before my eyes, a little sample of the knitter's art, a landscape in wool, and if anyone had told me this was the work of a blind person I wouldn't have believed it. At times I suspected she wasn't blind at all, but then she would start fumbling again in the sweater for her needles and carry on with her story, sometimes breaking off to concentrate on counting the stitches, feel along the edge, grope for the other strand—she had to work with two strands, sometimes even more—inserting the needles slowly but unerringly into the stitches, deeply absorbed yet looking beyond me, then resuming her knitting, without haste but also without hesitation. She would tell me about essential and incidental events, who and what had been involved in the invention of curried sausage: a naval petty officer, a silver equestrian badge, two hundred squirrel skins, twenty-four cubic meters of lumber, a whiskey-drinking, female sausage-factory owner, a British military commissary, and an English beauty with red-gold hair, three bottles of ketchup, my father, chloroform, a laughing dream, and much more. All this she told me in bits and pieces, postponing the end, boldly jumping back and forth in time, so that now I have to select, order, link up, and abbreviate.

My story will begin on April 29, 1945, on a Sunday. The weather in Hamburg: mostly overcast, dry. Temperature between 1.9 and 8.9 degrees Centigrade.

2.00 p.m.—Hitler's marriage to Eva Braun. Witnessed by Bormann and Goebbels.

3.30 p.m.—Hitler dictates his political testament. Admiral Dönitz to be his successor as head of state and supreme commander.

5.30 p.m.—British forces cross the Elbe at Artlenburg.

Hamburg is to be defended as a fortress, to the last man. Barricades are erected, the People's Army is called up, heroes are snatched from hospitals, the last, the very last, the very very last conscripts are thrown into the front, including Petty Officer Bremer, who had been in charge of the admiralty map room in Oslo. There he had been all but indispensable since the spring of '44, until he went to Braunschweig on leave. He stayed with his wife, had seen his barely one-year-old son for the first time, and could satisfy himself that the baby was teething and could say Papa. Then he had set out on the return trip to the admiralty marine map room. After reaching Hamburg in an overcrowded local train, he had been given a ride in an army truck as far as Plön and the next day by a horse-drawn wagon to Kiel, where he planned to take ship to Oslo. But in Kiel he was assigned to an antitank unit and, after three days' training in the use of grenade-launchers, was ordered to go to Hamburg where he was to report to his new unit, which was to be deployed for the final battle on Lüneburg Heath.

He had reached Hamburg about noon, consumed part of his rations—two slices of army bread and a small can of liverwurst—and taken a walk through the city. Although he knew Hamburg from earlier visits, he didn't recognize the streets. A few façades were still standing, beyond them the jagged, burned-out spire of St. Catherine's. It was cold. A cloud drifting from the northwest moved toward the sun. Bremer saw its shadow approaching him on the street, and it seemed to him like a dark omen. By the roadside, shattered bricks, charred beams, fragments of sandstone blocks that had once been the entrance to a building: part of the stairway was still intact, but it led into empty space. Only a few people were on the street: two women were pulling a small handcart; one or two army trucks running on charcoal burners drove past; a three-wheeled motorcar was being drawn by a horse. Bremer asked for directions to a movie theater. He was sent to Knopf's on the Reeperbahn. He walked to the Millerntor, then to the Reeperbahn. Hookers, gray and haggard, stood in doorways, their thin legs on display. The movie *Command Performance* was showing that evening. There was a long line at the box office. People had nothing else to spend their money on.

"Sorry," he said, apologizing to the woman standing in line behind him for having pushed her with his field pack.

"That's okay," said Lena Brücker. After finishing work at the food-rationing office she had gone straight home to change, and, since the sun came out from time to time between the clouds, she put on a jacket and skirt. That spring she had shortened the skirt a bit. Her legs were quite good—for now, she thought, but in three or four years she would be too old for such a short skirt. She had put some light-tan fake-stocking coloring on her legs, smoothed out the places that were a little too dark, then in front of the mirror drawn a fine black line down each calf. She had to take at least three steps away from the mirror, but then it did look as if she were wearing silk stockings.

At Grossneumarkt there was a smell of burning and wet mortar. The previous night a building at the Millerntor had been hit by a fire bomb: the pile of rubble was still smoldering. The bushes in the front garden had turned green from the sudden heat; those too close to the fiery ruin were withered, some small branches actually charred. She walked past the Café Heinze; only its façade remained. Beside the entrance a notice still read: SWING DANCING PROHIBITED! REICH CULTURAL BOARD. It had been a long time since anyone had bothered to clear away the rubble on the sidewalk. The bars were closed, no dancing, no striptease. She reached Knopf's Movie Theater, out of breath, saw the lineup, thought, I hope I'll get in, and took her place behind a marine, a young petty officer.

That was how Werner Bremer and Lena Brücker had happened to come there and stand one behind the other, and he had brushed her with his pack, a duffel bag with a rolled-up, gray-green-mottled army tarpaulin tied on top. "That's okay." It was only by accident that they got into a conversation. As she groped in her handbag for her wallet, her house key slipped out. He bent down, she bent down, their heads bumped, not hard, not painfully, and just for a moment he felt her hair, soft and blond, gently touch his face. He held out her key. What did she notice first? The eyes? No, the freckles: his nose was freckled, his hair medium blond. Could easily have been my son. But looked younger than he was, twenty-four at that time. She thought at first he was nineteen, maybe twenty. "He looked nice, so thin and hungry. Was so hesitant and not too sure of himself but with an open expression. Nothing else occurred to me. Not at that moment. I told him about the movie I'd seen the week before: *A Glorious Night at the Ball.* Going to movies was the only entertainment left, unless the power happened to fail again."

She wanted to know which unit he was serving with, and in asking the question she used the correct term. After all, one had been hearing and reading it every day: heavy units—the battleships, armored cruisers, heavy cruisers. Except that, apart from the *Prinz Eugen,* there was nothing left of the heavy units. But there were still some light units: torpedo boats, motor torpedo boats, minesweepers. And then the U-boats.

No, he had recently been on the admiralty staff at Oslo, marine maps department. He had been on a destroyer in 1940. Sunk in Narvik. Later on a torpedo boat in the English Channel, then a patrol boat.

They sat side by side in the creaking seats; it was

cold. She shivered in her light suit. The newsreel: Laughing German soldiers driving past on their way to repulsing a Russian attack somewhere along the River Oder. The preview of the next movie: *Kolberg.* Generals Gneisenau and Nettelbeck; the actress Kristina Söderbaum, laughing and crying. While the preview was still on—Kolberg in flames—the air-raid sirens began wailing outside. The house lights came on, flickered, failed. Flashlights glimmered. The audience pushed its way through the two exits and ran off toward the big public air-raid shelter at the Reeperbahn. To go into a public shelter was the last thing she wanted; she'd rather go to any private basement shelter. One of those mass shelters had recently received a direct hit in the entrance. A firestorm had swept through it. Afterward, people were to be seen hanging from the pipes, charred, small as dolls. Lena Brücker ran to an apartment house and followed the white arrow: AIR-RAID SHELTER, Bremer close behind her.

An air-raid warden, an old man with a facial tic, closed the steel door behind them. Lena Brücker and Bremer sat down on a bench. Across from them sat the building's residents—a few old men, three children, a number of women, their suitcases and carryalls beside them and draped blankets and quilts around their shoulders.

They stared at Lena and Bremer, probably thinking: Mother and son. Or: Lovers. The air-raid warden, in his steel helmet, was chewing as he looked across at them. And what's he thinking? There's another middle-aged woman who's picked up a young man. How those two put their heads together! The skirt's rather short. Shows a good bit of thigh. She's not wearing any stockings—where she had crossed her legs, the color had rubbed off, you could plainly see the bare flesh. But she was no hooker. Not even one of those amateur hookers. Their business was bad, very bad in fact. After all, there were any number of lonely women. Husbands at the front or killed in action. Women were throwing themselves at men.

The air-raid warden reached into his overcoat pocket and took out a small piece of black bread, which he chewed on as he stared across at Lena Brücker. Everywhere women, children, old people. And there sits a young fellow from the navy. The two of them sit there whispering. Must have met at a dance—a private one, of course, public dances were prohibited. No more public entertainment as long as fathers and sons were out there fighting. And getting killed. Every six seconds a German soldier is killed. But having a good time can't be prohibited, nor can enjoying yourself or feeling that urge to laugh when there's so little to laugh about.

The air-raid warden leaned forward, trying to listen in on the couple's conversation. But what did he hear? Headquarters, map room, marine charts. Bremer was whispering about navigational charts that had to be rolled, folded, numbered, and arranged alphabetically; he was in charge of them at Oslo, on the admiral's staff, and that meant having to compare or replace them with new charts.

It was vital not to make any mistakes, the charts must always be up to date. He marked them up with the positions of patrol boats, but above all of minefields, as well as the location of the entrances and safe passages. Or German vessels could run into German-laid mines—that had already happened. Not that he wanted to boast, but the job was quite important, and now, after spending his leave in Braunschweig, on his way back to Oslo, he had been assigned to an anti-tank unit. "You see," he said, "I'm a seaman." She nodded. He didn't say, I've no experience in ground warfare, it's pure madness. He didn't say: At the last minute they want to send me to the slaughter. He didn't say that, not only because as a man, especially as a soldier, you didn't say such things, but because it wasn't safe to say such a thing to a person you hardly knew. There were still people in Germany who went to the authorities to denounce defeatism. It was true he couldn't see a party badge on her jacket, but these days you didn't see them much anymore. They were worn under the topcoat, well hidden by a scarf.

Suddenly: a distant, dull roar, a violent shudder from the depths of the earth. "The harbor," said Lena Brücker, "they're bombing the U-boat bunker." Far off the rumbling of the exploding bombs. Then—close by—a detonation, an impact; the emergency lighting failed, another impact, the ground heaved, the building, the cellar, rocked like a ship. The children screamed, and even Bremer cried out. Lena Brücker put her arm around his shoulder. "Didn't hit the building, it was somewhere nearby."

"On a ship you see the planes, and you see the bombs falling," he said apologetically. "Here it comes as a bit of a surprise."

"You get used to it," said Lena Brücker, and let go of him.

The air-raid warden shone his flashlight on the steel door. The beam of light wandered over the people sitting there wrapped in their blankets as if they were snowed in. Chalk and dust went on trickling down from the ceiling.

After an hour the all-clear sounded. Outside a fine drizzle had set in. There in the street, only a few meters from the building, was the crater, three or four meters deep. Somewhere across the street the roof and upper floor of a building were on fire. From the ground floor women were carrying out an armchair, household linen, a grandfather clock, vases; on the sidewalk already stood a small round table with a pile of carefully folded sheets on it. Burning shreds of curtains floated in the air. What had surprised Bremer when he was in Braunschweig during an air raid was that people didn't weep, didn't scream, didn't wring their hands in despair, but, as in any ordinary move, carried their smaller possessions out of a building whose roof was on fire. Others walked by calmly, no, with indifference. An old woman sat in an armchair as if in her living room, except that she was sitting in the rain, a birdcage on her lap with a finch hopping around in it and shrieking while a second one lay on the bottom.

Lena Brücker turned the lapel of her jacket over her chest, saying, "I hope my building hasn't been hit." Bremer opened up his gray-green camouflage tarpaulin and arranged it carefully over Lena Brücker's head and shoulders. She raised the tarp slightly so that he could get under it too and put his arm around her. Like that, pressed close together, they walked through the now steadily falling rain without saying a word and, as if by tacit agreement, to her place on Brüderstrasse. There was no light in the stairwell, and they carefully groped their way up the stairs until he stumbled behind her. Then she took him by the hand, went ahead, unlocked her front door, and led him into the kitchen where she lit a kerosene lamp.

Mrs. Brücker puts aside her knitting, walks without hesitation to the living-room cupboard, which is of polished birchwood with a middle section of leaded brown panes. She gropes for the key that hangs from a tassel, opens the right-hand door, reaches into a shelf, pulls out an album, comes back, and lays it on the table. A photo album, bound in burgundy-red hessian. "Take a look. Must be a picture of the kitchen in there too."

On the first few pages the photos are neatly identified in white ink, the next lot are merely pasted in, the last ones lie loosely between the pages. "Is there a picture of that seaman?" "No," she says. I turn the pages: Lena Brücker as a baby on a polar-bear rug, as a little girl in a starched frilly dress, in a dark dress holding a small bunch of flowers after her confirmation, after that a baby wearing a knit bonnet and holding a teething ring, her daughter Edith, a boy on a scooter, a girl with her hair coiled in braids over her ears, looking up and holding two sticks joined by a string, obviously waiting for a Diabolo top that's not visible in the picture, a little boy with a teddy bear under the Christmas tree, Mrs. Brücker on board a motor launch, her hair blowing in the wind that presses her dress between her legs.

She has picked up her knitting again and is counting the stitches, moving her lips. A man on a motor launch. "Looks like Gary Cooper," I say. She laughs. "Yes, that's Gary. My husband. Everyone used to say: Looks like Gary Cooper! He was really good-looking. But he was also a pain in the neck. Women were always after him. And he was after the women. Oh well. He's been dead a long time now."

Then the photo of Mrs. Brücker in the kitchen. She is standing beside a young woman. Plump, freckled, I describe the woman. "You know her, she also lives in this building, Mrs. Claussen, downstairs, the wife of the dredge operator," says Mrs. Brücker, staring pensively at the wall. "What kind of a dress am I wearing?" "Dark, with little polka dots and a white lace collar, it's"—I hesitate—"rather low cut." She laughs and puts her knitting on the table. "Yes. My husband bought that dress for me. My favorite dress." Her hair, blond, is pinned up, spilling over the tortoise-shell combs on each side.

"In those days the only room I could manage to keep warm was the kitchen. Can you see the stove?" "Yes." "A small iron stove in the middle of the kitchen. The stove pipe has a bend in it as it goes through the room, then it leads out through the top of the casement window where the glass has been replaced with black cardboard. It was supposed to provide as much heat as possible. I could use the stove for both: heating and cooking. I also had a gas range, of course. But we seldom had any gas. The gasometer had been destroyed. I rationed myself very carefully, two briquettes a day, plus some wood from the rubble heaps. You could pick that up from the ruins, though only if you had a permit."

That evening she put in two extra briquettes, the ration for the next day. Never mind, she told herself, she wanted the place to be warm that night, really warm. She put on a kettle of water and shook a handful of coffee beans into the grinder. When did he have to join his unit the next day? Five o'clock at the main station. From there he was supposed to be taken to the front near Harburg. The British had already reached the other side of the Elbe. You could walk to the front. But they were to be transported by truck. The kitchen was warming up. He took off his pea jacket. On his naval uniform he wore two decorations and the Iron Cross Second Class ribbon, the Narvik shield, and a silver badge, one she had never seen before. The German equestrian badge. Surely that was something for the cavalry, the artillery, or, just possibly, for the infantry, but hardly for a seaman.

"My lucky charm," he said. Wherever he showed up with it, people laughed, just like she had, and that way he got into conversation with anybody. Both with superiors and subordinates. Iron Crosses, German Crosses, Distinguished Service Crosses, Knight's Crosses—after more than five years of war there was a glut of them, nobody was interested in them anymore; but an equestrian badge worn by somebody in the navy! People always asked: How ever did you come by that thing? And that was how he got the cushy job on the admiral's staff. Otherwise he would have been down among the fishes long ago.

He had served six months on a patrol boat, at the North Cape. "Monotonous," he said, "being on watch. Cold and dangerous. Torpedo planes were constantly coming across from England. That patrol boat was a converted Danish fishing vessel. Her diesel had already been rejected as obsolete by Noah when he entered the ark. The diesel invariably failed when it was urgently needed. Mostly in a storm. Then the waves would break across the boat amidships. Towering great devils they were. The pitching and tossing was beyond belief, and damn dangerous. I had to go below with the engineer to repair the diesel. The commander, a lieutenant from the reserves, was usually plastered. One time a bomber came, and we all thought, This is it, if it's going to fire torpedoes! But it only had bombs. I aimed the two-point-two flak at it. It crashed."

He pointed at the black-white-and-red ribbon in his buttonhole. Had he noticed that she was no longer paying proper attention to him? Heroic exploits didn't interest her, they never had, and certainly not after five years of war. Five years of victory fanfares, five years of special bulletins, five years: Gave his life for Führer, Nation, and Fatherland.

"Right," he said, "I'm getting off the subject. So, while we were lying off Trondheim the admiral in chief for Norway arrived for an inspection. We were all lined up. As he passes down the ranks the admiral stops in front of me. Looks at me and grins: 'Man alive! Do you ride across the sea? What is your civilian occupation?' 'Mechanical engineer, sir.' He gave orders to have me transferred to his staff at Oslo, where I was put in charge of the map room."

And when after a pregnant pause he tried to describe what he had seen from the patrol boat—how a ship had run into a mine, an explosion, the water was churned up, the steamer broke apart, the hissing of the fire in the boiler, the screams of the men in the icy water, how they drowned, but some who were wearing life jackets screamed and screamed, and when they fished out two of them and saw how their legs had been literally rammed into their bodies, those fellows died screaming he wanted to say, that was on his very first trip—Lena put the coffee grinder in his hands. She didn't want to hear anything about men drowning, freezing to death, being mutilated, she wanted him to grind the coffee; she didn't want to hear the story of the Narvik shield but only how he came by that entirely unmilitary and—to put it bluntly—only attractive badge. Presumably that hadn't cost anyone his life, at most the horse some sweat. "Wait a minute," she said, taking the coffee grinder from him and adding a few more coffee beans, more than she had ever taken at one time during recent months. She wanted to stay awake. An extra ration: ten days earlier there had been a special distribution. If it should come to fighting in the city, the population was to have enough provisions. He began grinding the coffee. She poured two glasses of her ferocious, home-brew pear brandy, seventy percent. Cheers. "That'll warm you up." A fellow worker had given it to her. She had a job in the canteen, at the food office.

"So you don't have to worry about food," he said. "Oh yes I do." Only once in a while was there a special distribution or occasionally something she could bring home from the canteen. Cheers. Did she have a radio, he asked?

Yes, but the tube was bust, and she hadn't been able to get hold of a new one yet. Besides, you couldn't listen that often anymore, only when the power happened to be on, and then it was always that Dr. Sedative. Sedative? Yes, Secretary of State Ahrens, the fellow who announces the unpleasant news over the radio. Gas consumption must be reduced. British terror-bombs have hit the gasworks. The German people will find other methods of cooking. Small home-made stoves. Dr. Sedative speaks slowly, in a quiet, subdued voice—no, gentle, soothing. Hence his nickname Sedative. No more power for the sirens, so our antiaircraft artillery will fire five rounds, signifying an air-raid warning. We won't let them get us down. But no more power means we can't hear Sedative anymore: Heroic resistance at the city's threshold.

They drank some coffee and with it a second glass of pear brandy. Was he hungry? Of course he was. She could offer him some mock-crab soup. A recipe she had developed herself. Something like mock turtle, she said as she tied on her apron. She had carrots and a stick of celery on hand, as well as some of the tomato paste that had just been delivered to the canteen. Fifty kilos of tomato paste out of the blue. She brought carrots, three potatoes, and a stick of celery from the storeroom, put a generous liter of water on the stove to boil, and began to scrape the carrots. Now then, how had he come by the equestrian badge?

He was from Petershagen, on the River Weser. His father, a veterinarian who kept two horses, had taught him dressage. Of course he used to go for rides in the countryside too, down to the Weser, where he would dismount and feel only one desire: to get out of that godforsaken place, as far away as possible, follow the flow of the Weser, to the sea. He obtained his intermediate school certificate, then, after an engineering apprenticeship, worked as an assistant engineer on a ship bound for India, just before the war. In 1939 he was drafted into the navy. After basic training he was assigned to a coast battery on Sylt. Nothing happened there, not a thing. Cleaning cannons. In the village there was a riding stable where, since he had all the time in the world, he successfully took the test for the equestrian badge. Shortly after that he was transferred to a destroyer. First trained as mate, then as boatswain. Served on the patrol boat.

Lena sliced the carrots into the saucepan, added the celery and three chopped potatoes, then spoke the magic words: "Celery, celery, cipprisa, cipprisapprisumm." After adding the boiling water to the vegetables she shook in plenty of salt. "There," she said, "now it has to boil till it thickens."

"My lucky charm," he said. At least up to now, for probably it was the equestrian badge that had given that officer the idea of assigning him to an antitank unit. "They tackle the enemy like the Mongolian hordes. Sheer madness." She was totally absorbed in pouring the coffee—how good it smelled. She watched the dark-brown foam welling up around the edges of the filter, the small, paler bubbles transforming themselves into fragrance.

"Did you go and see your wife?"

"No, I stayed with my parents, then later in Braunschweig. How about you? Your husband? Is he at the front?"

"I don't know," she said. "The last time I saw him was almost six years ago. He got drafted right away in '39. Met another woman, in Tilsit. He was stationed at a supply base. Writes occasionally."

"Do you miss him?"

What was she to say? She might have said—and that would have been the truth—No. But Bremer might have taken that for an invitation.

"Can't say I do and can't say I don't. He was the skipper of a motor launch, later a long-distance truck driver. But never mind," she said, "now he'll be somewhere or other. He'll survive. He's no hero. Most likely he's playing tunes on a pocket comb for the nurses. He's good at that. Can twist people around his little finger, not only women. But I don't care. Just so long as the government pays for the kids."

"Two kids?"

"Yes, a son, he's sixteen. With the air defense, somewhere in the Ruhr district. I hope the boy's all right. And a daughter, she's"—she hesitated, didn't say she's twenty, my God, twenty already, but "she's being trained," although Edith had finished her training as a medical assistant two years ago. "She's in Hanover."

"The British are already there," he said. "In Petershagen too. For them it's all over."

"I hope there was no raping."

"No, not with the British."

She watched him and saw from his expression that he was thinking; he's calculating, she thought, he's calculating my age. At this very moment he's realizing that I could be his mother; that look was directed not at her but only at a part of her, something on the surface. Annoyed, she turned toward the stove and stirred the bubbling mock-crab soup. She tasted it and, after adding more salt and some dried dill, said: "It'll be ready in a minute."

They had chatted, they had sat in a cellar, they had walked home through the rain under a tarpaulin. Nothing more. So far.

As she spoke, she was knitting the hill on the right

side of the sweater; from time to time—slowly—her hands would move along counting the stitches. Then the needles would start working again. I asked her what she had been doing in the canteen. Cooking? "No! I was in charge. Rustling up supplies and so on. I had been trained as a handbag-maker. Leather goods. Nice occupation. But after my apprenticeship I couldn't find a job so I worked as a waitress at Café Lehfeld." That was where she'd met her husband, Willi, whom everyone called Gary. She had waited on him, and he invited her for a drink. Naturally she promptly said No and asked him whether he thought he was the Emperor of China. "Sure," he said, then pulled out a comb from his pants pocket, wrapped a thin paper napkin around it, and began to play the theme song from *The Land of Smiles*. In the café all conversation stopped and everyone stared at them, so she quickly said Yes. "I became pregnant that very first night, though my doctor had told me that with my bent Fallopian tubes I couldn't get pregnant.

"Then after my second child I stopped working. During the war I was drafted to work at the canteen, first in accounting, then, when the Russian campaign started and the canteen manager was called up, I took over his job, kind of as his deputy. The food office is war-essential, so the canteen is too. The cook's good, a real wizard, from Vienna, his name's Holzinger, used to be a chef in Vienna, at the Erzherzog Johann. Really can make something out of anything. Spices, he says, that's what does it. Spices—on the tongue they're the memories of Paradise." She put plates on the table, opened a drawer and took out starched damask napkins that hadn't been used for at least two years, from the storeroom brought the bottle of madeira the office manager had given her for her fortieth birthday almost three years ago, and handed Bremer a corkscrew.

She placed three candles on the table. "Three all at once?" "Sure," she said, "no scrimping." From the storeroom she also brought the small piece of butter that was supposed to last three days and put it on his plate with three slices of rye bread. She ladled soup into his plate and sprinkled it with some parsley she had growing in a box on the windowsill. "Cheers," she said, and they toasted each other with the madeira, a wine so sweet that it gummed up Bremer's mouth. "Hope you enjoy this," she said, "but close your eyes!" Eyes closed, he obediently drank his soup. "You're right," he said, "it really does taste like crab soup!" He didn't tell her that just six weeks earlier, in Oslo, he had eaten lobster and shrimps, with horse-radish sauce. It really does, he thought, while trying to compare this flavor with the one of six weeks ago— maybe it was just his hunger, his ravenous hunger, he hadn't had a hot meal for three days, he mustn't gulp it down, he must savor it, eat slowly. Her gaze was penetrating. Yes, it tasted like crab soup, you had only to close your eyes, remotely it did taste like crab soup, only not so pungent, actually much better.

She had never liked cooking. Perhaps it was because of her father, who would sit there absentmindedly shoveling the food into his mouth. She had always tried to find a comparison until she recalled the watchdog she had observed as a child on her uncle's farm. That dog, when given its portion of tripe, would gulp it down mechanically. If it was disturbed, it would growl briefly, bare its teeth, then immediately go on eating.

She had cooked without enthusiasm for her husband, and without enthusiasm for herself—also, to be honest, for the children when her husband was not at home. But then, strangely enough, when there was a shortage of everything and other women lost interest in cooking because there were hardly any condiments or spices to be had, she suddenly started to take pleasure in it. She enjoyed managing with very little, experimenting with transferring flavors, and she tried out dishes which formerly, when spices were all still available, she would never have attempted. To make much of little, she would say, cook from memory. You knew the flavor, but you couldn't get the spices anymore, that was it, the memory of what was lacking; she searched for a word to describe that flavor: a remembered flavor.

They drank the wine and, because it was as sweet as a liqueur, interspersed it with pear brandy. "We'll both have a headache," she said, "but today that doesn't matter." "Yes," he said, "tomorrow is another day. If I'm going to have a headache it won't make a bit of difference, and not to the British tanks either."

For a moment she didn't know how to respond to that. Nothing, there's nothing to be said, she told herself, I should simply take him in my arms.

She told him that the hit tune, "Everything Passes, Everything Ends," was no longer allowed to be played on the radio. And why? Because everyone knows the new words: "Everything's collapsing, it's falling apart, first Adolf Hitler, then the whole Nazi lot."

It was warm in the kitchen, not so warm that she had to take off her jacket, but she was feeling very hot. She sat in her blouse at the kitchen table, and Bremer must have seen from close up what I could see in the photos: her rounded breasts. She poured him another pear brandy. The fellow at the office distilled this brandy in his allotment garden, secretly. He collected the pears in a barrel. In the otherwise silent night the 8.8 flak on the Heiligengeistfeld bunker fired once, twice—Lena Brücker was counting along—three, four, five times, the signal for the air-raid warning now that there was no more power. "Should we go down to the cellar?"

"No," he said.

She stood up—after a brief hesitation—she was already on her feet, took the first step and asked herself, What if he doesn't want to, if he takes fright, if he moves away, or even just winces a little, a mere twitch—then, what then? She went over to the sofa and sat down beside him. They clinked glasses with the rest of the madeira. I hope I won't feel sick, she thought, I hope I won't throw up. His cheeks were flushed with red patches, or maybe it was just her own. In the distance she could hear the antiaircraft shelling. No bombs were falling. "If you like," she told him, "you can stay." And later in the cold bedroom, in the massive white double bed in which she had lain alone for five years, she said: "You can, if you want to, stay here altogether." And she said that "altogether" as casually as if it were to be taken for granted. A vague word, and yet—she knew this—it was a word that would be decisive for them both.

He lay on her pillow, his arm under his head, and she watched the glow of his cigarette. "Do you ever have visitors?" he asked. "Sometimes. But no one I have to open the door to. This is an end apartment.

Hardly anybody comes all the way up here. And if they do, you can slip into the storeroom. I'll lock the door from the outside." For a brief moment his face brightened. From far away they could still hear the antiaircraft firing. The British were no longer bombing the bridges over the Elbe, the ones they had tried to destroy in past years. Now they wanted to take the bridges undamaged as far as possible. They were bombing the U-boats in the harbor. Then she noticed that he had fallen asleep, the burning cigarette between his fingers. She carefully removed it and stubbed it out. Lying beside him she looked at him, a shadowy figure, heard his breathing; it was regular. Gently she stroked his upper arm, the curve where the arm joined the shoulder.

At four the alarm clock went off, and he immediately jumped out of bed. She heard him go to the toilet, pee, and wash. He came back. She lay in bed, propped on one arm, watching him as, without saying a word, without a glance in her direction, he pulled on his gray underpants, his undershirt, his shirt, then his navy-blue pants. He walked through the apartment as if searching for something, opened the doors, looked into the storeroom, into the two big closets, and out the window down onto the dark street, of which only a short section was visible. The building across the street was somewhat lower. He stood there staring into the darkness, thinking about how two days ago they had assigned him to launching antitank grenades. A staff sergeant with the Knight's Cross, plus eight ribbons on his sleeve, which meant eight tanks knocked out with a hand weapon. A group of reservists, two members of a military band, two staff corporals, various clerks, a few marines, and a large number of Hitler Youths. "Easy as pie," the staff sergeant had said, "the antitank grenade launcher. You just have to stay calm and cool, let the tank approach to within fifty meters, then hoist the launcher onto your shoulder, sight your object, keep a good grip, hold your breath, and fire, but make sure no one's standing behind you, otherwise he'll be burned to a crisp."

Bremer had launched a grenade at a ruined wall. The grenade exploded in the designated area, pieces of brick were sprayed around. "Good," said the instructor, "the tank would now be scrap metal." Except that tanks didn't stand around in the landscape like walls. Tanks moved. There were usually several of them. And they fired. The closer they came, the more they turned into thundering, towering, gigantic steel monsters. So you had to learn how to dig a foxhole. The instructor showed them how to dig the kind of hole that was almost invisible to the tank gunners. How to arrange newspapers carefully around the hole and shovel the earth onto them so you could carry it away later. Dark, freshly dug earth, even traces of it, betrayed the position of the grenade launcher. It was on that spot that gunfire from the tank was instantly concentrated. And it was toward that spot that the tanks were steered.

It was only later, after the training session, when the Hitler Youths had gone home, that the instructor told the comrades from the navy what could happen when the tanks advanced. He had seen it happen to his friend, he said, as he drank some of the Danish aquavit that had been obtained from a derequisitioned food-supply depot. "There you are," he said, "sitting in that foxhole, and the tank drives over the hole and turns its right track, then its left, and digs itself in like that. So then you're sitting in the grave you've dug for yourself, watching the steel come closer and closer. So. Cheers," he said, "to that steel heaven."

"Come here," she said, and held out her hand to him. Bremer took off his pants, shirt, and undershirt, grasped the outstretched hand, and climbed into the swaying bed. That was how he, Hermann Bremer, a naval boatswain, became a deserter.

2

WHAT WENT THROUGH HERMANN Bremer's mind when he got back into bed again with Lena Brücker? Was it fear? Twinges of conscience? Doubts? Did he think, I am a swine, a traitor to my comrades? With each sweep of the second hand on the luminous dial of his watch, he was prolonging his AWOL as he lay there with his head nestled on Lena Brücker's shoulder, abandoning comrades who were now climbing onto trucks. Engines starting up, trucks rattling, the stench of diesel exhaust, and the men huddled on the floor inside, waiting. The first lieutenant glanced—like Bremer—at his watch, wait a bit longer. The soldiers sat there, silent, some smoking, some sleeping, their tarps pulled over their heads: armed civilians, marines, the two military band members. It was cold, and the rain was still falling. The first lieutenant raised his arm and climbed onto the lead truck. The four trucks drove off toward the bridges over the Elbe, toward Harburg and Buchholz, where children, women, and old men had already dug trenches—trenches that a few years later, as a boy together with some other kids, I used to scour. With a spade we would lift off some of the earth that had crumbled down into the trench, and we would find battered mess kits, water bottles, rusty steel helmets, cartridges, bayonets, and occasionally a rifle. Georg Hüller once even found an MG 42, known as the "Hitler saw," and another time an Iron Cross almost rusted through except for the silver edging. No shreds of uniform were attached to it, and there wasn't so much as a trace of a skeleton. The decoration lay among rusty belt buckles, snap hooks, gas masks, cartridges, and canteens from which a tealike brown liquid still dripped. Detritus of a war approaching its end. At this as at other lines, there was to be no final battle, merely a brief exchange of fire, one or two skirmishes, and the Germans, who had long ceased to form units, withdrew.

But Bremer couldn't know that. Bremer was scared; scared to stay with Lena Brücker, and scared to go to the front. These were his options: to desert and possibly face a firing squad of his own people, or go to the front and be torn to pieces by a British tank. In either case only one thing mattered: to get through alive. But which alternative offered the better chance? That was the question, and the search for an answer caused a restless tossing and turning in his head as well as in the bed.

Two weeks earlier, when he had come to the end of his leave in Braunschweig and was on his way back to Kiel, he found himself stuck in, of all places, Plön, where he had reported to military headquarters and shown his travel papers. In order to survive the war, particularly in its final phase when everything was disintegrating, the preservation of bureaucratic formalities became more and more important. It was necessary to prove when and how you were traveling, and where to, in order to avoid facing some drumhead court-martial. He was assigned quarters in the gymnasium of a school where a divisional staff was billeted. Early the next morning he was awakened by shouting, commands, nailed boots marching along the corridor. Picking up his shaving kit he went out into the corridor. How he hated that school smell, a smell of floor wax, sweat, and schoolboy fear.

In the corridor three soldiers were walking toward him, two carrying rifles, the one in the middle—a young man of maybe eighteen or nineteen—with his hands behind his back, and—Bremer noticed this at once—this man hadn't buttoned his tunic properly and there was a straw in his unkempt hair. The three men came closer, but not one of them—all privates—made any move to step aside for him, the boatswain, who was after all equal in rank to a sergeant, so that Bremer was forced to press against the wall to let them pass. The man—a boy, really—in the middle walked with his eyes on the ground, as if searching for something. As they were passing he raised his head and looked at Bremer, just one look, not frightened, not horrified, no, a look that seemed actually to drink Bremer in. Then the boy lowered his eyes again as if to make sure he didn't stumble. The hands behind his back were handcuffed. While Bremer was washing under a faucet that was much too low for him, having been designed for children, he thought, That's being wiped out now, whatever that look had retained—and that includes me. Later, while sitting on the toilet, he heard the volley.

With his head resting on Lena Brücker's soft shoulder, he mentally turned over the question: Stay in bed or get up? Shouldn't he try to hurry and join his comrades at the last, the very last moment? Not because he thought of his oath of allegiance or because it seemed to him degrading to simply duck out, but merely because he was weighing his chances of survival: Stay here and wait till the war is over, or slip away somewhere on Lüneburg Heath and then let himself be taken prisoner by the British, which, so he had heard, was far more difficult than you might imagine. You stepped from one organized system into another—hostile—one, and that could easily lead to misunderstandings, lethal. Or should he wait out the war here and risk being discovered and shot? Especially since from now on he was, for better or worse, dependent on this woman whom he had known for only a few hours.

Toward noon he was wakened by a driving pain in his head. He washed at the basin in the toilet, holding his head for a long time under the cold water. He put on his uniform. In the mirror he saw his reflection, the ribbon of the Iron Cross Second Class, the Narvik shield, and the silver equestrian badge. If he were to be discovered now, he thought, that badge would be of no further use to him. He had done something final: in other words he had, strictly speaking, done nothing. I have gone off in one direction, and I can no longer turn back in this attic apartment—he would not be able to leave until the British had taken the city.

Standing at the kitchen window he looked down through the net curtain. Below was a quiet, narrow street devoid of green and, intersecting it, a narrow lane. From time to time he saw women walking along carrying pails, empty, on their way down the street; when they returned, water slopped out of the pails. So there must be a hydrant on the street. Once an elderly soldier passed by, a reservist wearing gaiters over his laced boots, bread bag and water bottle hanging from his belt. He was shuffling along, stooped, flat-footed, and pigeon-toed at that. On his back he carried an old-fashioned carbine: if Bremer was not mistaken, a captured Polish carbine. A captain approached in the opposite direction, and the two met more or less in the middle of the street. The reservist merely raised his hand briefly, not even as far as his cap, a casual gesture, a mere hint of the military salute it should have been. And the captain, in his long gray overcoat, fitted at the waist and probably custom-made, didn't give the man a dressing down, didn't say: You will kindly stand at attention, my man, the flat hand is brought to the edge of the cap, touching it lightly, the edge of the hand is to be at an angle of seventy degrees, and so on—no, the captain walked by and merely nodded. But in his right hand he carried a string bag containing potatoes. A captain carrying potatoes in a string bag on the street: There could be no doubt—the war was lost.

How quiet the city was. Sometimes he heard voices. Children playing. And from time to time, in the distance, artillery fire. Over there, in the southwest, was where the front was. Then he noticed the woman. She was standing in the entryway of a building, a young woman in a brown coat. What struck him about her was her pale silk stockings, something rarely seen in the sixth year of the war. Flesh-colored silk stockings.

Walking through the apartment, Bremer stopped

and looked at the living-room cupboard: inside were a few crystal wineglasses, ruby red. A table with chairs of dark stained wood. The furniture wouldn't have been out of place in any large, expensive apartment. A wooden rack contained a number of magazines. He leafed through them, saw photographs of events that had occurred months, years, before. Tanks outside Moscow. Lieutenant Commander Prien with the Knight's Cross at his neck. Dr. Sauerbruch visiting a field hospital. Bremer found some crossword puzzles and began working on one. At intervals he would get up and look down onto the street. The woman was still standing there. Children ran past, and more and more women came with pails, empty as well as full. Occasionally a man: once it was a private first class on a bicycle, probably a dispatch rider. After more than an hour the woman went away. Two women, one old and one young, were pushing a two-wheeled cart laden with pieces of splintered wood from the ruins.

Bremer read an article on the Afrikakorps. The magazine was three years old. A report from a distant world. German soldiers were frying eggs in the African sun on the steel plates of their tanks. One picture showed General Rommel standing under some palm trees. German troops advancing on the Suez Canal. *John Bull is tottering,* said one caption. A wounded British soldier being bandaged by a German stretcher-bearer. In the background a destroyed tank with dark smoke belching from its hatch. Now John Bull has reached the Elbe, thought Bremer.

Hearing the sound of a motor, he ran to the window. Down below, an all-purpose army vehicle was driving past at walking speed. In it sat three SS soldiers. The vehicle stopped. The driver beckoned to a woman and spoke to her. The woman pointed this way and that. And then at the top floor of the building where he stood behind the window. The vehicle slowly backed up. It was the moment, as he later told Lena Brücker, when panic almost made him dash out of the apartment. But then he had asked himself in horror whether there was a rear exit to the building; for all he knew, the SS men would already be coming up the stairs as he was running down. That had given him the crazy notion of escaping to the attic, climbing out through a skylight onto the roof, and standing on the rain gutter while climbing to the sloping roof. And on top of all these hectic thoughts racing through his head came another, a suspicion, the craziest of all which only now, when she was here, had proven to be that crazy. Actually it had been the most obvious one, he said—that Lena had denounced him to the police, out of fear, out of mortal fear, since anyone who hid deserters was shot or hanged. Or, said Bremer, someone had noticed him last night going into the building with her, someone who hadn't been able to sleep and, like himself a while earlier, had been looking out the window. In his mind's eye he still saw a woman standing at a window, staring into the dark street; saw himself arriving with Lena under the tarpaulin and entering the building. He had listened at the apartment door. The stairs in the building creaked under hesitant footsteps. But no, in the stairwell everything was quiet. Only from below, very far away, could he hear a few voices. He had stood by the window for a long time, and when nothing moved, and there was no sound, he calmed down, telling himself that it had been a coincidence that the woman had pointed in the direction of this building. He went back to the kitchen window. From time to time he saw the woman and children with their pails, people walking by. And from a distance, coming from Wexstrasse, he could hear the motor of a military truck.

It was the same kind of truck that Lena Brücker had waved down early that morning. The truck stopped; men from the Luftwaffe were sitting in the cab with a woman between them. Where to? Eimsbüttel. Jump in and join the fun! the driver said. Lena Brücker climbed in. Hardly had the truck started than a confused groping of hands began: the assistant driver, a private first class, was kissing the woman, his hand up her skirt. Her right hand was somewhat mechanically stroking the soldier's thigh, that horribly scratchy gray uniform material, while her left hand disappeared into the driver's open fly. Meanwhile the driver, when not having occasionally to change gear, was likewise busy with his right hand under the skirt. When the other soldier, without looking, groped with his free hand for Lena Brücker's knee, she grasped his wrist and said: "I'd rather not." Suddenly the three of them stopped, just for a moment, smiling and fully understanding, not in the least angry or reproachful. The assistant driver and the woman looked at Lena Brücker before getting busy with each other again. A gurgling laugh, heavy breathing, squeals. "I kept thinking, Let's hope he doesn't hit a lamppost, he drove slowly but rather jerkily. Even made a detour and, like a taxi, dropped me right outside the office."

Mrs. Brücker laughed and for a moment let her knitting rest on her lap.

"Yep," she resumed, "as far as that goes, I was never prudish but I was always picky. Never lacked for offers. But," said Mrs. Brücker, "either the fellows were so coarse and crude, grabbing at you right away, or they had a smell I don't like—in those days, believe me, men smelled stronger, of cheap tobacco, cold food and grease, and of course there wasn't much soap. Or they looked at you with eyes like the neighbor's dog. I was free, after all. Husband away. Didn't have to ask anyone or consider anyone's feelings except my own. But only once during those six years did I go with a man. It was New Year's Eve 1943. A few of us from the office had got together, a bunch of women as well as the few men who'd been exempted." She had danced a long time with a man who was in charge of flour distribution. A good dancer who could waltz to the right as well as the left and, even when she felt a bit giddy, held her firmly and securely—she could lean back and tilt her head way back. Till the man couldn't go on and was panting. At midnight they all raised their glasses, and someone called out: "A happy New Year and a peaceful one!" After that she had danced several more times with him, close together and slowly, though she would really have preferred to dance nice and fast. But he couldn't go on— he had asthma. And then she had gone with him to his place, cramped, temporary quarters. He had been bombed out, and his wife and four children had been evacuated to East Prussia. He was living in one room that had a sagging double bed in it.

When it was over she felt sick to her stomach, not from self-disgust, there was no reason for that—the man was a kind, shy asthmatic. She had already noticed him earlier in the canteen. On humid summer days he would drink a lot of water and sometimes pump air into his mouth with a little rubber ball. During the night she had woken and found the man beside her, breathing heavily and snoring. She was stone-cold sober. Next to her lay the wheezing body of a stranger. She had gotten up, quietly left the building, and walked through the night from Ochsenzoll to her home. It took her three hours, the long and exhausting walk she needed to gradually shift the events of the night into the distance. As if she had conducted an experiment on herself the outcome of which was dissatisfaction. She could think calmly of that, but what really bothered her was the thought of the first day at work in the new year when she would meet the man again. His first look at her turned out to be exactly what she had expected: meaningful, obtrusively intimate, stupidly familiar.

She had tried hard not to react aggressively toward him. She made a point of avoiding him, had seen to it that there were always others around when she could no longer avoid him: a complicated web of questions, summonings, inquiries, while he stood there looking at her, expectant—no, reproachfully sad. Until one day he intercepted her on the street outside the office and asked what was the matter.

What he had done wrong. Nothing. It had all been so nice, hadn't it?

"Of course," she said. "Let's leave it that way."

"No, it wasn't nice," said Mrs. Brücker. "Or rather, for one moment it's quite nice. But before and after, no, it wasn't. I was quite free, after all, and yet it was a kind of betrayal, of myself if you like. Perhaps I'd have done it more often if the men had vanished when it was over, simply been swallowed up by the ground. As it was, though, whenever you met them each gesture, each smell, each look would also be a reminder of what you hadn't liked about them."

"And Bremer?"

"Not with Bremer. I liked him right away. Why do we like a person? I mean, before they even open their mouths. Right off. Not this feeble getting-to-know-each-other. The very sound of that gives me the shudders! Love through familiarity. What rubbish. So boring. With Bremer it was different, quite different."

Hugo came into the room, the conscientious objector with a ponytail and gold earring, white-coated, pushing a small cart. Its rubber tires squeaked on the gray vinyl-covered floor. On the enamel top of the cart stood little jars, boxes, and bottles containing ointments, tablets, syrups.

"Ah, here comes the old folks' chow," said Mrs. Brücker. Hugo shook three pink pills into her palm, went over to the kitchenette, and came back with a glass of water. "With Hugo's help I manage to stay on here," she said. "They want to shove me off into the nursing department. But I always say: Without a cookstove a person isn't worth a thing. Once I wanted to make Hugo a curried sausage, but of course he'd prefer kebabs."

"Not really," said Hugo, "if it has to be fast food, I'd rather have a pizza."

Hugo picked up the front part of the sweater: The background was light brown, in a valley some blue had gathered from the sky, and the dark-brown trunk of a fir tree on the right reached high up into it. "Super," he said, "perfect by the time there's more sky and the branches of the fir tree in it. I'll be looking in again later."

"Did you get the curry powder from the canteen?" I asked, to get her back on track again.

"The curry powder? No, there wasn't any of course. It was wartime, don't forget. No, it wasn't that simple." She picked up her knitting and fingered the edge, counting stitches, silently, then murmuring 38, 39, 40, 41. She began to knit. "That first day I could hardly wait to get home. I put on my smock and went to the canteen kitchen. Holzinger was already waiting. 'We have to make it fish today,' he said. 'The official district speaker's coming for a visit. Intends to deliver a pep talk.' Holzinger had worked for years at the Erzherzog Johann as second sauce chef and later as first sauce chef on the liner *Bremen*. He must have been an inspired chef, one who today would surely be running a two-star restaurant. At the start of the war, Holzinger was called up for duty at the canteen of the Reich radio station in Königsberg. 'The mind,' Goebbels had said, 'needs first-class menus, otherwise it is uninspired, carping. An empty stomach sharpens every doubt. Flatulence, heartburn, turn every shadow pitch black. That is why propaganda centers must employ good cooks. No profession is as easily seduced by good food as that of workers of the brain.'"

Holzinger was put in charge of the Reich radio station canteen. A few months later, several radio announcers and editors suffered attacks of vomiting and diarrhea, strangely enough always when military victories were to be reported. The victory over France was celebrated, flags were flown, marches were played, flowers were strewn along Sieges-Allee in Berlin; the Führer with his cornflower-blue eyes reviewed the parade, but the commentator of the Reich radio station was kneeling at the toilet and throwing up. Since the same thing had happened when the victories over Denmark and Norway were announced, and again after the capture of Crete and Tobruk, suspicion pointed at Holzinger. No one had ever heard a critical word from his lips, a fact that served only to reinforce the suspicion of deep-seated treachery. There exists—I have had it played to me—a recording of a live broadcast in which the announcer starts to gag at the words "our victorious paratroopers"; after the word "Crete" comes an acoustic gap, the microphone is briefly switched off by the announcer, then comes a belched "captured" followed by sounds of vomiting. End of broadcast.

When the report about the victorious German mountain troops scaling Mount Elbrus was scheduled to be announced, but couldn't be since the newscaster lay writhing with stomach cramps on the editorial sofa, Holzinger was ordered to report to Gestapo headquarters. He cited the food supplies delivered to him: after all, he couldn't sterilize lettuce, or buttermilk either, by cooking them, could he? And then there was the water. There were, Holzinger pointed out, many cases of vomiting and diarrhea in the city. He had himself suffered from stomach cramps at the same time as the announcer. The Gestapo official was convinced. Holzinger was sent back. He was temporarily confined to quarters and sworn to secrecy about the interrogation. He was dismissed from the radio station and transferred to the food office in Hamburg. No one, not even Holzinger himself, could tell why he had been transferred specifically to Hamburg.

Three weeks after Holzinger started work, Mrs. Brücker was summoned to Gestapo headquarters. A Gestapo official told her that she had been proposed for the position of manager of the canteen. He asked her whether she had noticed anything in particular about Holzinger, whether he had made any derogatory remarks about the party, about the Führer? No, nothing of that kind. Was the food good? Holzinger was a wizard, Lena Brücker said, he could make something out of almost nothing, and something excellent out of anything. And how did he do it? His secret was the way he used spices. The official, a pleasantly quiet young man, pensively chewed his lower lip. She was to let him know if Holzinger made any defeatist remarks. Was she a party member? No. Hm. The man bound her to silence. With that she was dismissed. She told Holzinger that she had been questioned about him. From then on she invariably ordered fish when the district speaker Grün was expected, as he was that day. Grün's father owned a fish shop, and more than once Grün had emphasized that he couldn't even smell fish without feeling nauseated.

The reason was that as a boy he had had to grab the fish out of the fresh-water tub, then stun them with a blow to the head, slit them open, and clean them.

Lena Brücker telephoned the fish market and was told that not a single fish had been caught. No more fishing boats were coming up the Elbe because the Tommies had already occupied the other side of the river. She called the off-rations market, and they had several kilos of tripe. The previous night bombs had fallen in Langenhorn, one, a parachute mine, right beside a farmyard. The barn was still standing, but the windows and doors were gone. All the cows lay there dead, intact, and quite appetizing. Only their lungs had been ripped out of their bodies.

"Tripe, we can get twenty kilos of tripe."

"That's fine," said Holzinger, "we'll make chitlins. We've plenty of potatoes in store."

Lena Brücker set the tables for the executives. She did that personally. There were even still some paper napkins. Six months earlier, a supply for the next thousand years had arrived. The napkins were also used as toilet paper.

At noon, all the food office employees gathered in the canteen. Mr. Grün the speaker, who looked sallow in his brown uniform, arrived with the general manager, Dr. Fröhlich, also in his brown party uniform, tall, soft brown leather boots, starched tan shirt, gold cufflinks, immaculate. The speaker didn't pull any punches. He contrasted European culture with the Jewish-Bolshevist perversion. Here wholeness of thinking, there division, destructive criticism. Positive, negative. So: confidence and courage determine German thinking. By contrast, vacillation, faultfinding, defeatism are something Jewish. Then from Grün's very mouth, comparisons: Leningrad and Hamburg, Moscow and Berlin. At this they all pricked up their ears, yes, he was saying it openly: At one time the Russians had seemed done for, but then they had defended Leningrad, encircled for three years; the Russians had defended the city tooth and nail and had turned a disastrous defeat into victory. And we shall do likewise. Grün promised final victory by observing that when a man has been knocked down, if it is his home turf he can defend it far better because he knows it so well. That is how Hamburg will be defended, street by street, building by building. The shirker, the coward who slinks away, is a traitor to his people, repulsive, a source of infection that must be cauterized. The common will. The British are going to be surprised at the fanatical resistance that will confront them. And for that it is important that this office, being responsible for the distribution of food, also does its part so that each citizen receives his due share. Strength, strength for the final victory:

that is what ration cards stand for. And then Grün quoted Hölderlin, not for Lena Brücker, who merely organized the canteen, matched the distributions against the ration cards, checked the dish-washing, set the tables for the executives. No, he quoted Hölderlin for the special benefit of all the department heads, business executives, lawyers, and political economists. So that their minds might become elevated and, in line with the seriousness of the situation, their purpose firmer yet. *Sieg Heil!*

The speaker sat down and wiped the sweat from his brow. Dr. Fröhlich stood up and promised that this department would do its duty until final victory— supply the population with food. Moreover, if necessary the office would be defended by force of arms. He then joined Grün and the other leading citizens at the canteen table. Lena Brücker waited on them. Grün said he would soon have to leave, he had to give a speech in half an hour to the employees of the Habafa battery factory. They must all work for victory, one last, final effort.

"Whatever you do, don't touch anything from the tureen at the head table," Holzinger had said. "I would like to spare our fellow workers at Habafa a speech." It was the only time Holzinger gave a hint of his kitchen sabotage. Lena Brücker spooned the chitlins onto the district speaker's plate and heard:

"Hang on, fine, but fight of course, antitank weapons, obviously, but what a wonderful smell!" he said. "Chitlins, ahh, and caraway seed, ahh!"

"So many ahhs, but also so many buts," said Mrs. Brücker, "that struck me at the time, they were new. 'Schnapps is schnapps, and duty is duty,' said a counselor at the table. But if those two had been more closely combined, things might not have become quite so disastrous."

Suddenly Grün sprang to his feet and, with his hand to his mouth, rushed out of the room. Dr. Fröhlich, gagging, hurried after him.

Dressed in his naval uniform, Bremer sat at the kitchen table and waited. He looked as if he was about to get up and leave, sat there as if in a waiting room.

He stood up, went toward her as if she were returning from a long journey, put his arms around her, and kissed her: first her neck, her chin, then the place—he didn't know this yet—that gave her goose pimples on her shoulder, behind first her right earlobe, and then her left. He had just shaved, she could feel that, brushed his teeth, she could smell that. He had put his tie on carefully, unlike her husband, who wore one only when he left the apartment and then always yanked it out of his collar as soon as he came home. He helped her off with her coat and began to unbutton her dress, until—in her impatience—she pulled it off over her head.

Later, while she was putting the potatoes on to boil in the kitchen, he read to her out of the newspaper, which by now consisted of a single sheet: Breslau is still fighting, Russians have encircled Berlin, heavy losses in street fighting, German troops have for tactical reasons again withdrawn before British and American divisions. A temporary postal worker had been beheaded with an ax for stealing parcels addressed to the fighting troops.

Reports from the Harburg front. Near Vahrendorf, troops were engaged in combat. In the approaches to Ehestorf, stubborn fighting erupted. As always, the enemy suffered a large number of bloody casualties. Our own losses were of course minor.

There was no mention of the Borowski group. Borowski, one of whose legs had been sawed off by a machine-gun volley. Nor of the seventeen killed in a shell hole in which Bremer, who had been assigned to the Borowski group, would probably also have been lying this very morning.

Instead he could light the cigarette that Lena Brücker had brought him. "Fabulous," he said, leaning back on the sofa, "just like Christmas, yet it's already May." With her ration card she had bought a pack of Overstolz from Mr. Zwerg who was pretty much surprised, knowing as he did that she had quit smoking six years before and since then had been exchanging her cigarette coupons for food, in fact with my Aunt Hilde.

Mrs. Brücker briefly counted her stitches. "Your Aunt Hilde was a heavy smoker."

I told her I could clearly remember having my first curried sausage at her stand with my Uncle Heinz, who was actually only my step-uncle. Was it true that he could detect the origin of potatoes by their flavor?

She muttered again, held her finger on the precise spot where the dark-brown trunk of the fir tree grew out of the light-brown earth, took the dark-brown strand, knit seven stitches, then, taking the light-brown strand, said: "It's true. At that time Heinz was on the eastern front, it ran through Mecklenburg. He was a potato connoisseur, the way other people are wine connoisseurs. He could tell the origin of potatoes by their taste. And what was most amazing was that he could do this even when the potatoes were boiled, fried, or mashed. He could even tell which field they came from, just like other people can taste vineyards.

"He would let himself be blindfolded: 'These potatoes in their jackets came from the Glückstädter Wildnis. This mashed potato was at one time the famous Soltau Grenade, a potato like a rock, very heavy, firm but never waxy, or the Buxom Alma, delicately floury as it melted on the tongue, to be found only in sandy heath soil. Those little potato cubes in turnip soup (with cubed pork), they are Bardowiek Truffles, a small dark-brown variety, firmer to the bite, tasting of—yes, of black truffles. And then the incomparable Bamberg Crescents.' Bremer had found it hard to believe this, so I told him: 'Just wait till he's back again.'"

That "just wait" led to a pause, to his being visibly taken aback. It had simply slipped out, that "just wait," but it was a giveaway that she was thinking of the future, probably even planning it. Something, Mrs. Brücker assured me, that she hadn't had in mind at all. At least not consciously. "It was simply like this: Two people sit together, talk, and feel comfortable, and you want it to stay like that. Never thought of the future, of living together, let alone of marriage—after all, I was still married. To be together, no more than that, but no less either. While he was only waiting to get out of the apartment, at long last to get home."

So she immediately tried to play down those words by saying, as she set the table: "Oh well, whatever happens it won't go on much longer. I hope Heinz will come back in good shape." And smoothly changing the subject she told him what the district speaker had proclaimed that day to the assembled staff. Hamburg will be defended. To the last man.

"Madness," said Bremer.

She pricked the potatoes; they were still not quite done. "How long can a city be defended?" "Long enough," replied Bremer, "for no stone to be left on another. Leningrad was defended for three years, the difference being that here the Tommies will deploy their bombers. They don't have to fly very far these days. They'll start from Münster, Cologne, or Hanover. And what we have here, these aren't troops anymore, just old men, paper pushers, military band players, Hitler Youth, amputees—nothing to put on a show with. That's it—show!" he exclaimed as he jumped up. "That's the word I needed!" and off he went into the living room to enter it in his crossword puzzle.

Just then the doorbell rang. For a moment they stood there petrified. "Quick! Put away the plate, the spoon and knife! The glasses!" The bell rang again, longer, more insistently. "Just a moment, I'm coming!" she called, pushing Bremer into the storeroom while from outside someone was knocking on the front door—not just knocking but banging, hammering. She runs into the bedroom, picks up Bremer's things, his cap, sweater, socks, throws them all into the storeroom where Bremer is standing, pale, rigid; the ringing becomes persistent, hammering on the door, "Hello there!" a man's voice calls out, the voice of Lammers, the block and air-raid warden. "I'm in the john," she calls, tiptoes to the john and flushes, knowing that Lammers is listening at the front door, tiptoes to the sink where Bremer's shaving kit is lying. Where to put it? Into the laundry bag. She locks the storeroom door. "Hello there!" comes Lammers's voice. The letter flap in the front door is raised, fingers, then Lammers's voice calling through the letter slot: "Mrs. Brücker! I know you're there. Open the door! I can hear you. Open the door at once! Open up!"

"Coming! Just a moment!" She unbolts the door.

In the storeroom Bremer has carefully sat down on a trunk and, like a child in hiding, peers through the keyhole into the corridor: a pair of laced boots, black—one, the left, smaller, humped, an orthopedic boot—above them leather gaiters, a gray, threadbare army overcoat, an air-raid helmet and a gas-mask container hanging from the belt. An old man's voice says he has to check the blackout in the apartment. Asks whether the pails are filled with sand. "For all we know, an incendiary bomb might drop on the building," says the voice. "Or a shell," she says, "the British are already firing across the Elbe." But Lammers doesn't want to know about it. "We're firing back!" "That I can't hear," says Lena Brücker. "They're being thrown back. Have you any doubts about that? Hamburg is a fortress. Are you smoking again?" asks the voice, and Bremer thinks he can hear an ostentatious sniffing. "Yes, a relapse." "I heard it from Mr. Zwerg," says the threadbare army overcoat. "You're picking up cigarettes again on your ration card. You used to always exchange them for potatoes, didn't you?"

"So?"

And then Bremer sees the boots, the overcoat with the helmet and gas-mask container, disappear into the kitchen, followed by Lena Brücker. Lying on the kitchen table is Bremer's lighter, a 20-millimeter flak cartridge converted into a cigarette ligher engraved in Norwegian. Although she had noticed the lighter when he lit his cigarette, she had paid no further attention to it. But now it lies there like a display piece from a war museum. A brass object, highly polished from use, round, long: a cartridge. Lammers is staring at it too. She takes a cigarette from the pack, concentrates on not letting her hand tremble, picks up the lighter, heavy and smooth it lies in her hand. She flicks, flicks again. The little wheel is stiff. Then, at last, comes the flame. Lammers has been watching her. In his face she sees a brooding suspicion. Her hand has trembled a little, hardly noticeably, but to her it had seemed to be shaking violently. She draws carefully on the cigarette so she won't have to cough. She had stopped smoking nearly six years ago, when her husband was called up. And effortlessly at that, as if with his disappearance she had also lost the desire to smoke. "A captured enemy lighter," Lammers says. "Yes, from Normandy, a gift." Lammers tries to decipher the inscription. "Not French," he says. "Course not." "Polish?" "Don't know." "Smells good here." "Yes." "Meat? Meat!" She sees those hungry old man's eyes, full of suspicion but also of greed; the pinched, sexless mouth struggles against the flood of saliva. She stirs the pan of chitlins. "I'm sure I heard voices," says Lammers. "Is your son here?" "What do you mean?" she says. "You know he's with the air defense, in the Ruhr—that's to say, he's probably been taken prisoner. The Ruhr army has surrendered, remember?"

Of course Lammers noticed that she was trying to draw him out of his stiff-necked reserve by quoting names—Normandy, Ruhr army, lost battles—but it was this very attitude that led to the lost battles, the attitude of: You go on shooting, comrade, I'll go for some grub, all that critical, skeptical, demoralizing talk. Sloppiness everywhere, in the factories, at the front, even on the home front. Demoralizing jokes: What's the difference between the sun and the Führer? The sun comes up in the east, the Führer goes down in the east. Silly jokes. Shells that fail to explode, torpedoes that go off course. The usual routine sabotage on the home front, even among those closest to the Führer, sabotage that has led to the enemy setting foot in our own country.

Lammers stumped to the window, examined the blackout shade, twitched it, and said: "There's a tear here, light can get through. Things like this can give the terror bombers their bearings." "That's impossible." "What do you mean?" "When do we ever get any electricity?" Then he bent down to peer under the kitchen table. "What are you looking for?" Lammers told her that people in the building had complained. "What about?" "Cries, at night." He looked at her. I hope I won't blush, she thought, but of course she did, I can feel it, the flaming heat rising up from my entire body, all my blood collecting in my face. "Why? I'm a poor sleeper. Wake up at night, sit up in bed and cry out. No wonder, really," she said, "with the British just outside the city." "What are you trying to tell me?" Lammers asked. "What do you mean, *I'm* trying? It's in the paper, right here. You can see where the front is." She held the newspaper out to him.

Bremer saw the laced boots coming out of the kitchen, the gaiters, the army overcoat, closer, closer, until all he could see was gray, then again the belt, the steel helmet, the boots. Lammers bent down in the hallway over the three sand-filled pails. "Are you in any doubt that the city will defend itself?" he asked. "No. Just today I heard District Speaker Grün's speech." Lammers went into the living room, then the bedroom, and when he knelt down—somewhat laboriously, first on one knee, then on the other—to peer under the bed, Lena Brücker said: "That's enough—there doesn't have to be a fire swatter or any sand under there."

"Hm," he said, "I'll see to it that you get some people billeted here. Two rooms and a kitchen for a single person, and out there thousands of our citizens are on the street, bombed out or refugees."

"Do you mean to say that the Führer hasn't conducted the war successfully?"

He hesitated, aware that a trap had been set for him to stumble into. "If your son is here, you'd better report it to the police. Otherwise I'll do it. And then you'll both be in trouble." Lammers limped across the hallway again. "What's this smell?" Bremer could see him standing in the hallway sniffing. "A smell of leather, of barracks. As an old soldier I know that smell."

"Out," said Lena Brücker, "get out, and make it snappy!" She slammed the front door after him, just catching the heel of his orthopedic boot. Leaning back for a moment against the door, she could hear him clumping down the stairs, muttering angrily, but could make out only isolated words: "Barrage, Kyffhäuser, Verdun, put the fear of God into them." Now it's all over, she thought, he'll go to the Gestapo, he'll denounce me and say I'm hiding someone in my apartment.

She went to the storeroom and unlocked the door. Bremer emerged, pale, sweat on his forehead although it was ice-cold in there. As he stood there, she could see, in spite of the wide-cut navy trousers, that his knees were trembling. They went into the kitchen and sat down. And, looking straight into Bremer's anxious, no, terrified face, she said: "That was Lammers."

She propped her elbows on the kitchen table, held her head in her hands, and laughed, a forced laugh that was very close to a sob.

"Lammers is the block warden, lives in the next building, used to work at the land registry office, now he's a pensioner and air-raid warden." She removed the potatoes, meanwhile boiled to a mush, from the stove. Bremer said he'd lost his appetite, but then he did eat, rapidly, including her portion, only pausing now and again to listen, as she did, for sounds in the stairwell. Then he went on eating. "Tastes good," he said, "simply fabulous."

"Funny," said Mrs. Brücker, "isn't it, when something was good, I mean specially good, Bremer would say: fabulous. But he couldn't really enjoy those chitlins. He was still scared stiff. And I couldn't eat a thing—after all, we couldn't be sure Lammers wouldn't come up again. Besides, because of the fire hazard, he had a key to my apartment, so he could come in any time I was at work. Lammers wasn't only the block warden, he was also the air-raid warden. He had joined the party rather late, but then with a vengeance, a one-hundred-and-fifty-percent believer. At Verdun he had been wounded in his foot by a shell splinter and claimed that an angel, not a Christian one but the soul of his deceased great-aunt, a farmwife, had diverted this shell splinter—actually meant for his head—to his foot. This great-aunt, you see, had a clubfoot. People laughed at Lammers. He believed in the transmigration of souls. Told everyone he could remember a previous life when he had been a captain in the Bavarian artillery and in 1813 had marched under Napoleon to Moscow. He had been drowned during the crossing of the Beresina. He saw himself riding across the frozen river when a cannonball struck the ice beside him, splintering and ripping it open, and he and his horse both plunged into the black icy water. The horse's neighing and his own death cry still rang in his ears.

"Everyone called him our snowman—only when he wasn't around, of course. And everybody laughed at him, until 1936, that was when Henning Wehrs was arrested in the next building. Wehrs was a ship-wright at Blohm und Voss and till 1933 had been a member of the German Communist party. When Wehrs got drunk on Fridays, he began blasting away at the Nazis: Gang of murderers was the mildest. Everyone told him: For God's sake, shut up! If that ever got to the wrong ears! And then one day there was a ring at the door. Mrs. Wehrs opens. Outside are two men asking if they could have a word with Mr. Wehrs. And since Henning Wehrs had just come home from the early shift, had just washed up and put on a clean shirt, he could go along with them right away. The three of them went down the stairs, talking about the weather, the Elbe, which was very low, and walked to the municipal offices. It was three weeks before Wehrs returned. Wehrs was Wehrs, yet no longer Wehrs. The man whose laughter could be heard through two floors, who cracked jokes about that fantasist Lammers and then laughed at them louder than anybody, didn't laugh anymore. It was as if that laughter had been stolen from him. Like in a fairy tale: Wehrs wasn't injured, had no bruises, no bleeding fingernails, no needle marks, nothing, but he didn't laugh anymore, and wouldn't say why. He had simply, as Mrs. Brücker put it, lost the power of laughter. A somber silence. Didn't laugh, didn't swear, didn't weep. Looks like a zombie, said someone in the building. Even his wife couldn't get a word out of him. From that time on, he never touched her. Lay in bed, awake, sometimes he would groan. And another thing: he didn't snore anymore. Sometimes in his sleep he would scratch the side of the bed, which invariably woke her up, it was such a piercing sound, Mrs. Wehrs told people at the dairy and began to weep.

"What's the matter? What did they do to you?"

"Nothing," he said.

On Fridays he drank. But now in a quiet way, and so much that he had to be led home. Once he said: "One has to have seen that." What? But he wouldn't say *what* one had to have seen. Then one day he plunged from the slipway where he had no business being. He was killed instantly. The word was that he had committed suicide. His wife received a pension. Industrial accident: His workmates had testified that he'd had to replace a steel brace up there. At the time there was a rumor that Lammers was the one who denounced Wehrs. Lammers had just joined the National Socialist Party. That was all. No one could give a concrete reason for the rumor, yet it persisted. On the street they said: "It was Lammers." People stopped greeting Lammers, or did so cursorily. When he went into a store, all conversation ceased, or they talked with conspicuous loudness about the never-ending rain, or the sun, or the wind. Without being asked, Lammers told everyone he hadn't denounced Wehrs. People turned away. Almost tearfully he would protest that he could never do such a thing. But then, six months later, when he was still surrounded by that silence, he suddenly began asking those who fell silent near him, in the stairwell, at the butcher's, in a restaurant, for their opinions. Not indirectly either, but point-blank. "Do you think it's right that the synagogues were burned down? Would you buy from Jews? Hide a Communist?" People answered evasively, but he remained stubborn, refused to be put off, so they gave answers, agreeing hesitantly, tortuously, and they heard others lying and heard themselves lying. So once again Lammers was greeted, at first slowly and tersely, then—Poland had been overrun by the Wehrmacht—affably, then—Norway and Denmark were conquered—with marked affability and, when France capitulated, almost enthusiastically. Some who didn't greet him, or who did so reluctantly, were summoned to the Gestapo, which questioned them about where they had obtained the schnapps for a recent party. In 1942, when the Jewish Levy Foundation on Grossneumarkt was evacuated, they greeted him with raised right arms, shouted "Heil Hitler, Mr. Lammers!" even across the street.

Lammers was made block warden; Lammers organized the evacuation of children to the country, the Winter Relief Campaign, and later the air-raid precautions. On account of his injured foot he had retired two years early, quite unnecessarily because he was in good shape, visibly in good shape, in fact he was getting in better and better shape all the time. No wonder, for the sausage was weighed at the butcher's in such a way that the saleswoman could ask, "Mind if it's a bit over?" which, since sausage was available only on ration coupons, she had no right to do. The baker still had some rolls for Lammers long after they had become unobtainable. Only Lena Brücker, known as a stubborn Schleswig-Holsteiner, consistently greeted him with: "Good morning, Mr. Lammers." And each time Lammers would say: "Heil Hitler is the German greeting, Mrs. Brücker." "All right, Mr. Lammers, Heil Hitler." One day she was summoned to the Gestapo, but there she was questioned about Holzinger, with whom Lammers had no connection.

"Maybe you should have offered him some chitlins," said Bremer. "He could smell the food through the doors."

"Nothing doing!" said Mrs. Brücker. "That fellow's never going to put his feet under my table! He must've become suspicious because I wasn't in the cellar last night during the air-raid alarm. Normally I always go down. Thinking of the kids. I hope the boy's all right. And Edith, I wonder what she's doing? We have to be extra careful. Don't move around too much. But above all when the doorbell rings, lock yourself into the storeroom.

He couldn't fall asleep. As always, she lay on her stomach, on her breasts like little pillows, and slept. Carefully he slipped his hand onto her plump hip. He lay there quietly, glancing from time to time at the luminous dial on his watch and waiting for daylight to return at last, at long last.

3

LENA BRÜCKER WAS IN THE CAN-
teen telephoning for spring carrots to make sure the
food distribution organizers received the vitamin re-
quirements, while the radio was reporting the last, the
very last, but at the same time increasingly crucial
evasive withdrawal and regrouping action by the
German troops. Bremer had just gotten up, put his
pea jacket over his shoulders, and was looking down
from the window onto Brüderstrasse. Like yesterday,
women carrying pails were coming and going, some
quickly, some slowly: from the way they walked, from
the slanting shoulders, the careful footsteps, he could
tell whether the pails were full or empty. But the
hydrant where they got the water was out of sight.
The sun was shining, yet the people down there
looked gray and depressed. The women were still
wearing their dark winter coats, their hair hidden under head scarves. An old man was pulling a little cart
on which lay a few charred boards and, perched on
top of the boards, a chicken.

Bremer sat down at the kitchen table and drank
some of the acorn coffee Lena Brücker had kept
warm for him. The coffee puckered his mouth; it

contained only a hint of real coffee. She had put out two slices of bread for him and some margarine, made into a fancy shape like in a hotel, two cloverleaves. And beside it was some homemade apple jelly. He ate the bread, lit a cigarette, and drank the coffee which, strangely enough, had a stronger coffee flavor when you inhaled. He started on a new crossword puzzle. A city in East Prussia, six letters: Tilsit. That city no longer existed. A literary genre beginning with N, seven letters. He didn't know. A Greek poet with H, five letters? Homer. Now and again he moved to the window and looked down. Women were still lugging water, others passed with empty pails, and for the first time he saw the end of the lineup where the women were waiting. So that's where the hydrant was, just out of sight. Kids were playing hopscotch. Again he saw the woman he'd noticed yesterday, only this time she was wearing black silk stockings. A corporal came up and spoke to her. She crossed the street with him, disappearing from view. A few minutes later she appeared at a window across the street. In the background stood the man, unbuttoning his tunic. With a flick of her wrist the woman closed the curtain, and a shadow pulled a dress over its head.

At noon, when the power came on for two hours, he checked the cord of the radio, which stood on the kitchen counter, pressed down the two knobs, hit the box three or four times with the palm of his hand and finally with his fist. Out of thousands, hundreds of thousands of "people's radios" throughout the rest of Germany, where talk about "holding out," about realignment of the front lines, or merely hit tunes were being broadcast at this very moment, out of all those radio sets this one had to be on the blink. He could have listened to the BBC, and he would know the actual position of the Allied troops. He unscrewed the back of the set. The tube had turned black. If he could find an old set in the apartment, he could take the tube out of it.

Going to the living-room cupboard he hesitated, telling himself that there certainly couldn't be a radio tube in there. He searched in the storeroom, among shoes, cartons, mothballed winter coats, two battered cardboard suitcases, a largish carton marked "Christmas tree ornaments." Back in the kitchen he looked into the cupboard and carefully sorted the random array of pots and pans. Arranged the cans labeled Flour, Sugar, Semolina, neatly in one row. Except for the one marked Flour, they were all empty. He had long since stopped looking for a radio tube: now he was rummaging inquisitively in every corner of the apartment, looking for traces of her, of her life, which he did not know. While admitting to himself that what he was doing wasn't very nice, he decided it would be useful to have an atlas so he could accurately follow the advance of the British troops, and that was a reason to go on searching, even in the living-room cupboard, with not quite such a guilty conscience.

The shelves on the left contained crockery, those on the right files, family documents, insurance cards, birth records, Lena Brücker's confirmation certificate: "Be thou faithful unto death, and I will give thee a crown of life." For a moment he hesitated, then went on rummaging, one or two bundles of letters, beside them a photo album bound in red hessian. And under it lay the school atlas.

He pulled it out but then began, as I was to do many years later, to leaf through the photo album. Lena Brücker as a baby on a polar-bear rug, as a little girl in a starched frilly dress, as a teenager with a wreath of flowers in her hair, black stockings showing up below her short skirt, a young man at her side. A striking feature of these pictures, consisting as they do of mere shadows, is her shining blond hair. A photo taken at a party: she looks daring, her face is radiant as she sits there with a little paper hat on her head, a paper streamer around her neck, sunk back in an armchair, which makes her legs—modestly side by side—appear even longer, her skirt has slipped up a bit, the top of her stocking clearly visible.

Lena Brücker carrying an infant in her arms, supporting its head; she has rolled up the sleeves of her smock. He thought of his son, whom he had seen for only twenty days, a child who began to squall when he tried to caress it. And to tell the truth, that child, which claimed a great deal of time for itself, had interfered with his leave. Not that he had hated the child, but he was conscious of something he was at first reluctant to admit to himself, of an impatient annoyance because his wife constantly had to attend to this child, because it had to be diapered, washed, powdered, or simply picked up. It screamed at night, constantly, until she took it into their bed, which meant placing it between herself and him. To be honest, he had to admit to being jealous of this child. Bremer turned some more pages and found the man who must be Lena's husband: A tall, slender man, in a suit, smoking, one hand, the left, casually resting on his hip, like a movie actor.

Bremer put aside the album, whereas later I continued to turn the pages, looking at Mrs. Brücker's children, the boy in a Hitler Youth uniform, finally in the uniform of an air defense helper. Then the loose pictures, which at that time Bremer couldn't have seen: the daughter with the grandson, the son as a chimney sweep beside his VW. Pictures from the fifties and sixties. Mrs. Brücker over the years, the skirt now longer, now shorter, the shoes now with platform soles, now with stiletto heels, then suddenly those featureless department-store dresses of the sixties, no low neck, no tight waist, although she had a good figure, spray-cemented blond curls where the gray was apparent only to someone like me who had seen her hair in its natural state. She doesn't look fifty, more like forty, yet something has vanished from her face, some capacity for enjoyment, the lower lip, that sensually prominent lower lip, has become narrower, shows little creases.

Bremer went on rummaging: insurance policies, electricity and gas bills, a packet of letters tied with blue-and-red string. The sender's name: Klaus Meyer. For a moment he hesitated, then untied the packet and read the top letter:

"Dearest, I am sitting in my room at the inn Zur Sonne, and from downstairs, from the restaurant, I can hear them playing cards. I wish you were here now. We would have had supper together, fried sole fresh-caught from the Elbe, and drunk some red Spanish wine, supplied via Glückstadt, and we would have come up here. The wind is pressing against the windows, and from the Elbe, like the moaning and groaning of the earth, come the sounds of a dredger.

"This morning, at the local notions shop, I sold two packages of brass navy buttons and a dozen mother-of-pearl buttons, that was all. But after that I went to see Junge, the old boat-builder. He could actually draw me a picture of a jib tackle-ring. . . ."

Strange, thought Bremer as he put the letter back, wondering whether he should read another one, but then he tied the letters up again, telling himelf that he could never write such a letter. Like the moaning and groaning of the earth. Actually the earth really was torn apart by dredging. Who was this Klaus Meyer? He would never be able to ask her.

Bremer went into the bedroom. The shelves on the right-hand side of the cupboard contained neat piles of men's shirts. Next to them hung three suits, one dark blue, one light gray, one brown. He put on the gray suit and stood in front of the bedroom mirror. The suit was a little too big. The man looking at him out of it was a stranger: after all those years in the naval uniform, now in light gray. This motor-launch skipper knew how to dress. What was amazing was the quality of the cloth. Surely motor-launch skippers don't earn that much, he thought. The suit smelled of lavender. In each pocket he found a little bag of lavender. So she was still expecting her husband. If he were to come through the door, he would have only to reach into the cupboard and pick out a shirt. Bremer put on a pale-blue shirt, then the gray suit, and chose a flame-patterned blue tie. He looked older, no, more sedate, in this suit. And unmistakable. Anyone seeing him would be bound to take him for a successful businessman or a very young lawyer.

At that moment he heard the knocking at the front door, a gentle, amost diffident knocking. Snatching up his uniform, he hurried—he could already hear the key grating in the lock—into the storeroom, locked the door, and pulled out the key. He tried to calm his breathing, his panting, more from fear, inner turmoil, and holding his breath than from the hasty movements and the few steps he had to run. Had he forgotten something? Mightn't one of his socks be lying around there? Or his belt? No, he had that in the storeroom. He looked through the keyhole in the storeroom door and saw the orthopedic boot, saw Lammers in his gray army coat, saw him limp carefully into the kitchen. Bremer could hear a scratching, grating sound. What was he up to in there? Then Lammers walked past again and into the living room, where the school atlas lay open. There was nothing suspicious about that. Suddenly the coat came closer, until the keyhole was all black; then, very gently, the handle was turned, and Bremer involuntarily recoiled. There was a pulling at the door, a rattling. Footsteps moving away. Bremer could distinctly hear Lammers opening the door of the bedroom cupboard. Lammers went into the bathroom, more precisely only a toilet with washbasin. And then it flashed through Bremer's mind: His shaving kit was lying there. Lammers would find a shaving brush, a razor, and a piece of soap—dry, since he hadn't shaved since yesterday, yet obviously the shaving kit had been used recently. Lammers came out of the bathroom, limped along the corridor, and gently closed the front door behind him. Bremer waited in the dark storeroom and, hearing nothing more, emerged, went into the bathroom, and saw: The shaving kit was gone. Lammers must have taken it with him.

He'll be back, thought Bremer, he'll be back with an army patrol, they'll take me away. Should he simply go out onto the street? But there every policeman would ask for his identification, a smartly dressed young man, not in uniform—that was unheard-of. His one chance, he thought, his one tiny chance, was to tell them when they came: I am a Swedish seaman. He sat down again in the storeroom, and heard the blood surging through his head.

That evening Lena Brücker walked up the stairs; as usual, the stairwell light remained on only until she had reached the third floor. She was just about to walk up the last flight when an apartment door opened, and Mrs. Eckleben came out saying: "There's someone in your place."

"No!"

"Yes, there is. I keep hearing footsteps, right above my living room."

"Never!" said Lena Brücker. "That's quite impossible!"

"There *is,*" insisted Mrs. Eckleben, "I was about to call the police, I'm quite sure: someone's walking about. You'd better get Lammers before you open the door. Suppose there's a burglar in there?"

"Of course!" cried Lena Brücker, giving her forehead an exaggerated slap. "Of course, I quite forgot about my friend—I gave her the key."

"Didn't sound like a woman's footsteps."

"That doesn't surprise me—she's a crane operator at the dockyard."

"Well, I suppose you know what you're doing." The door closed on an Eckleben face stiff with suspicion.

Lena Brücker unlocks her apartment door and quickly closes it behind her. She goes first into the kitchen, then into the bedroom, "hello?" she says softly, and, just as she heads for the living room, the storeroom door opens and out comes her husband.

"What are you doing here?" she tries to ask but is too terrified to get a word out. Only as he slowly emerges from the darkness does she recognize Bremer. "Lammers was here, in the apartment. I must clear out. He made off with my shaving kit." Now she can laugh and tell him she had put it in the laundry bag the day before.

"You're bristly today," she says when he kisses her. Then she points to her husband's black shoes that have been in the storeroom for six years, that she had not touched in all that time. Nor the suits, nor the shirts, which she had washed, carefully ironed, and then neatly put away. She had kept them because, though she wasn't all that superstitious, she thought, If I give away his things, he's sure to turn up one of these days, to claim them. Then she would have to explain why she had given them away. And then he'd simply stay on, and she would be in his debt. Only the underpants and undershirts, those she had given to the Winter Relief Campaign. For this she had a ready excuse that her husband wouldn't have been able to refute. The piles of unused underwear had helped the fighting troops shivering in the Russian winter. Besides, he would never ask about the underwear, which simply always lay there freshly laundered and wasn't worth mentioning, she being the only one dealing with dirty underpants. There was always a chance he might turn up and ask for the expensive tailor-made suits and shirts, or for the shoes with "Made in USA" stamped on the leather lining. It always irritated her that all these items of clothing were out of keeping with the district, with this building, with this cheap, cramped apartment.

"They fit," said Bremer, taking a few steps.

"You mustn't walk about in shoes. Mrs. Eckleben was about to call the police, she thought there were burglars here."

She took out a packet of rice from her string bag. An extra allocation that day.

"Yep," said Mrs. Brücker, "and then he asked me whether I happened to have any curry powder." Mrs. Brücker laughed. She picked up a new stitch, from time to time that quick fingering to the edge. "Christian, my great-grandson in Hanover, will soon be graduating from high school. He loves to ski. This sweater is for him. He's Heinz's son. Heinz is Edith's son, she's my daughter.

"I'll make us some coffee." She stood up slowly, went into the kitchenette, and turned on the heating coil, then shook some coffee into the filter and groped for the pot. "Can I help?" I asked, thinking she might scald herself, if only from a splash of the boiling water.

"No, I can manage." She poured the boiling water into the filter, took a piece of ripe Gouda from the refrigerator, cut it into small pieces, and put the plate on the table.

I tried to bring her back to the curry.

"So it was Bremer who discovered the recipe, was it?"

"Bremer, what do you mean?" "Because he asked." "Asked what?" "Well, about curry." "Oh I see. No. What happened with the curried sausage was an accident, nothing more. I stumbled. That's when it happened. One big mess it was, too."

"Did you have any curry powder in your kitchen back then?"

"Of course not. Nowadays people cook and eat all kinds of things from all over the world—spaghetti, tortellini, nasi goreng or whatever all that stuff is called. Here for example they serve curried veal. Turkey with curry. That's what I like best. But they only make it every two weeks. Sad to say."

She brought the coffeepot, felt for the cups, and poured, both cups almost equally full. She drank and listened. Nothing to be heard but a distant stir, a hum against which now and again an isolated sound stood out, a door banging, the elevator starting up, voices, footsteps squeaking on the textured vinyl floor.

Using a fork she skillfully separated bite-size pieces from her marzipan torte; for each new morsel, she felt her way with the fork to the end of the slice of cake. She actually sucked each morsel, and as she sucked an expression came over her face, a capacity for enjoyment that made it possible to understand something one wouldn't normally associate with this bent old woman: a voluptuous pleasure detached from her will, an enjoyment that transformed her whole body. Then I saw the ill-fitting dentures that shifted as she chewed, and I thought of injury and the word prosthesis.

"Tell me about the curry and Bremer."

"When Bremer saw the rice he asked whether I had any curry powder, if so he could make some curried rice."

"What made him think of curry?"

"Just before the war Bremer had worked as second engineer on a boat going to India," she says, pushing a piece of marzipan torte into her mouth. She chews. Savoring in silence. Then she eats a little piece of the Gouda. "The boat, the *Dora* she was called, was lying off Bombay. And Bremer, just eighteen at that time, was suffering not only from a terrible heat rash on his face, red, with pustules, but also from homesickness. The first officer took him ashore for a meal, curried chicken, that tasted, Bremer said, like a garden, a taste from another world. The wind; the snake that bites; the bird that flies; the night, love. Like in a dream. A memory of when we were once plants. And that night Bremer actually dreamed he was a tree." "A tree?" "Yes. Bremer was more of a, let's say, down-to-earth kind of person. But then he began to get quite lyrical. Said the wind had gone right through him, he had rustled, and he had felt such an all-over tickling sensation that he had to laugh with each gust of wind, so much so that his branches hurt him. Then he woke up, and his sides actually hurt, here in the ribs. He showed me, giving me a gentle little dig in the ribs. Crazy, isn't it? It's the spice for depression and sluggish blood. The rash had gone, you see. A kind of food for the gods, Bremer said. It was the only marvelous thing Bremer ever experienced. Otherwise nothing but murder and mayhem."

"Did you make the rice with curry?"

"There wasn't any, remember? I cooked the rice with a bouillon cube and added some finely chopped glazed onions. After the meal Bremer lit a cigar, one of the five genuine Havanas that Gary had left behind in little metal tubes, screwed tight, but by that time they were dry as straw, their wrappers flaking. After lighting up, Bremer had to blow out the little flame burning at the tip of the cigar as it was about to incinerate the whole cigar in his hand. 'Go to the john,' I told him, 'you can smell it all over the building. If Lammers smells a cigar, he'll be here like a shot.' So Bremer went off to the john and opened the little window."

Lena Brücker put the plates in the sink and went to the storeroom to get a broom. There on the floor, beside the trunk, where he had left his uniform jacket, she saw a wallet. Some of the photos, papers, marching orders, his paybook, had slipped from it and fanned out. He must have simply thrown his jacket down on the trunk. She picked up the papers and the wallet, meaning to put them back. On spotting a postcard-size photo she went to the lamp: Bremer in uniform holding a small child in his arms, beside him a woman, dark-haired, with coal-black eyes and a little dimple in her chin. The baby Bremer was holding was less than a year old. He and the woman looked as if they were about to burst out laughing. The photographer must have cracked a joke. She stared at the picture. She also found a date written on it: April 10, 1945. He had never said anything about a child, or a wife.

"I wondered: Why would anyone deceive such a pretty woman? Why had he said nothing about his wife? Even if he'd told me, I would still have hidden him. Maybe also slept with him—for sure, in fact. But everything that came after that wouldn't have happened the way it did without his concealment."

When he came back from the john after a good half hour, smelling of cold smoke, when he took her in his arms and led her by the hand into the bedroom, when he put his big hand inside her blouse, she suddenly seized his hand and held it in a vise-like grip. "Ow!" he said. Pushing him slightly away so she could look into his eyes, she asked: "Tell me, do you have a wife?" After a slight hesitation he answered: "No." She shook her head and laughed a little, an artificial laugh, and stood still so that his hand wouldn't tear another button off her blouse, and she told herself that actually she had no right to ask him. He kissed her neck, the dimple, the salt cellars, which was what her mother had called the little hollows at her neck; then—as if he knew what sent shivers down her spine, what gave her goose pimples—the place behind her earlobe, and they sank into the creaking, sagging mattress. The springs squeaked until there was a knocking from below. Someone was banging on the ceiling. "Mrs. Eckleben," panted Lena Brücker, out of breath, "she sleeps directly underneath."

They pulled the mattresses, which in those days were still in three sections, off the swaying double bed, carried them into the kitchen, and laid them down beside the sofa.

It was the first time they had slept on the floor, and since the kitchen was warm they didn't need to pull the quilt up over their noses. "Love consists of accommodating," said wise Mrs. Brücker, "and I'm now referring to that new resting-place, thinking it's quite a different feeling when, as you lie under your partner, you don't sink into squeaking depths."

An island of mattresses pushed together, that's what it was, although, just when you were moving violently on them, they tended to drift apart. So much so that they had to devise something to prevent this nuisance. They first laid a blanket on the floor, then the mattresses on top, pushed them against the kitchen cupboard, supported them against one wall with a broom and a mop, pushed the sofa against the head end, and wedged the whole thing with two chairs against the wall so that the mattresses couldn't shift about.

Bremer regarded the mattresses with a sailor's expert eye and said: "Looks like a raft."

"On which we'll drift till the war's over," she said, "so come, my hero," and pulled him down beside her on the mattress raft.

4

ON MAY 1, 1945, RADIO HAMBURG announced: This afternoon, at his command post in the Reich Chancellery, the Führer Adolf Hitler, fighting Bolshevism to his last breath, gave his life for Germany.

The city commandant of Hamburg, General Wolz, wants to surrender the city without resistance; the British have crossed the Elbe and are marching on Lübeck; Field Marshal Busch gives orders to hold out; Grand Admiral Dönitz gives orders to hold out. Wolz dispatches parliamentarics. Secretly because the SS executes parliamentaries. District Leader Kaufmann wants to surrender but daren't say anything because he doesn't know whether City Commandant Wolz, who also wants to surrender, wants to surrender; and Port Commandant Admiral Bütow wants to surrender but likewise doesn't dare say anything because he doesn't know whether Kaufmann and/or Wolz want to surrender or only one of them or neither of them. So each works independently of the other on the surrender of the fortress of

Hamburg. Wolz pulls the reliable—but for his purpose unreliable—troops out of the Harburg front, transferring them to the northeast: the SS combat group *Panzerteufel*. All three—Wolz, Kaufmann, and Bütow—provide themselves with reinforced staff guards, so that officers in favor of holding out cannot arrest them. District Leader Kaufmann lives in the fortress of Hamburg in a fortress within a fortress, surrounded by barbed wire. During the morning, rallying cries are broadcast, and weather reports, even the water level is measured, one meter above normal. In Eutin, three marines who had gone AWOL are executed. Just outside Cuxhaven a British tank is destroyed; the crew dies in the flames.

Immediately after the news of Hitler's death, Holzinger had ordered pea soup, the Führer's favorite dish, to be served on May 2. The trumpets of Jericho, ha ha. The previous day Lena Brücker had learned that an SS provisions depot near Ochsenzoll was being dismantled, and she had managed to acquire twenty kilos of dried peas as well as a side of bacon. Lena was setting the table for the department heads when someone burst into the canteen shouting, "Listen to this!" as he switched on the loudspeaker. On the radio the voice of District Leader Kaufmann: " . . . *is making preparations to attack Hamburg on the ground and from the air with its vastly superior*

forces. For the city, for its people, for hundreds and thou-
sands of women and children, this means death and the
destruction of the last-remaining means of existence. The
fate of the war can no longer be reversed; but fighting in
the city will mean its senseless and total destruction."

"A bit late in the day to realize that," says Lena Brücker, "but not too late yet," and takes off her smock.

The announcer reads out a declaration: "All vital means of communicaton will be secured. People of Hamburg, show yourselves to be worthy Germans! No white flags to be hoisted. Hamburg's security forces will continue their duties. All black-market activity will be ruthlessly prosecuted. People of Hamburg, stay in your homes. Obey the curfew." Lena Brücker picks up her carryall, which contains a pot of pea soup, and says: "Well, so long!" Thus, for her, the Thousand Year Reich comes to an end.

Hurrying home, she calls out to people she passes: "The war's over! Hamburg is being surrendered without resistance!" No one she met has heard the appeal. They were still afraid there would be street-fighting, as in Berlin, Breslau, and Königsberg. Buildings flattened by mortars, stubborn fires, bayonet-fighting in the sewers.

But then, at Karl-Muck-Platz, it occurred to her that she'd also have to tell Bremer: The war's over—

Hamburg has capitulated. When I tell him he will, she imagined, first be taken aback, then, if he's sitting down, he'll get up and, when he's standing, raise his hands, his expression will change, his eyes, those pale-gray eyes, will darken, he will look so happy, yes happy, little creases will form around his eyes, creases that are visible only when he laughs. He might grab hold of me and whirl me around the room, he'll exclaim, "Wonderful!" or, more likely, "Fabulous!" There's something childlike about him when he's happy. And his listening is childlike, too, that surprised, "You don't say!" when I tell him something. He'll stay on for the time being, champing at the bit, for no one could go out on the street yet. There was a twenty-four-hour curfew. The trains wouldn't be running. The British would be in control of the streets. He would be here, but already no longer here. No matter what he was doing, he would be poised to leave at any moment, leave for Braunschweig. That's how it is, she thought, can't be helped; it was, when she thought about it, like a shadow that showed her future life without illusion. It was a stage in her life from which normally she would have almost imperceptibly slipped away. It had been such a short time, only a few days, yet with it something in her life had definitely come to an end. She couldn't say her youth, for after all she was no longer young: no, after that she would be old. And perhaps it was just this calm certainty that triggered an alarm, yes, a rage in her, the notion that he would borrow her husband's suit. A perfectly natural and understandable wish but one that nevertheless roused her to indignation.

He would say: "I'll send it back as soon as I can. I'll send a parcel," he'd say, "as soon as it's possible to send parcels again." He would think of her, but always in connection with that nuisance of having to take a parcel to the post office. A suit that was waiting to be folded, which probably his wife would do, carefully padding it with tissue paper, if she had any. He would take the parcel to the post office. He would tell his wife a story. He would say that after the surrender he had borrowed this suit from an army friend. He's no good at lying because he's no good at telling stories. He's only good at keeping things to himself. That he's good at. Her husband could lie because he was wonderful at telling stories. So Bremer would tell a thin story, maybe something like this: At the last moment he and a comrade had managed to separate themselves from their unit. He will give him a name, Detlefsen, from Hamburg, living in an apartment in Hamburg near the harbor, a naval diver. They had gone into hiding there. A wife who could make wonderful mock-crab soup. No, she thought, he won't mention me, or maybe—but she quickly pushed this thought aside—say his friend had a mother who was an excellent cook. No, she hated the thought of that, she hated the very idea of this parcel; she thought, he hasn't lied to me directly, he just didn't tell me he's married. But she hated this parcel and the idea that, if he thought of her in the future, it would be in connection with this parcel.

She unlocked her front door, did not call out: In Hamburg the war's over. Finished. Over and done with. She merely said: "Hitler is dead." For a fraction of a second, she told me, she had hesitated, had wanted to say, The war's over, here in Hamburg. But he already had her in his arms, was kissing her, had pressed her down on the sofa, that sagging sofa. Perhaps I would have told him later. It would've been easy, but then he said: "Now we're going for the Russians, joining forces with the Yanks and the Tommies." And he said: "I'm as hungry as a bear."

She placed the pot of pea soup on the stove to heat it up.

"Somehow he had inquisitive hands," she said, "no, not unpleasant, on the contrary. He really was a good lover." For a moment I hesitated, wondering whether one could ask this woman, who was almost eighty-seven, what she meant by a good lover.

Might I ask her a personal question? "Go ahead." "What do you mean by a good lover?" She paused briefly in her knitting. "He took his time. Knew how to spin it out. And he could do it often. Well," and then she did hesitate slightly, "also in different ways, know what I mean?" I nodded, although she couldn't see that; and although, as I readily admit, this "in different ways" interested me, so did—I'd be lying if I denied it—*how* often. I didn't ask. But what I did ask about was whether she had had a guilty conscience at not telling Bremer anything about the surrender.

"Yes, I did," she said, "I did, in the beginning." The first few days it had been a constant struggle not to simply blurt out he truth. And of course later, but that was another story. "But in the middle, kind of, not really. No, I enjoyed it, yes, enjoyed it, to be quite honest. Yet I've never liked lying. It's a fact. Telling fibs, sure, now and again. But lies, my mother used to say, lies make the soul sick. But sometimes lying heals, too. I suppose I kept something back, and he kept something back: his wife and child.

"Yes," she said, "he walked around in his socks. The war in Hamburg was all over, but he still walked quietly around in his socks. There was no more fighting, and I had someone in my home who crept around in socks. Not that I made fun of him, but I found him comical." She laughed. "If you find someone comical, it doesn't mean you have to stop liking him, but you can't go on taking him all that seriously."

Next morning she walked downstairs. At the bottom stood Lammers, the block warden, solemn as a judge: "Adolf Hitler is dead." He didn't say: The Führer is dead. He said: "Adolf Hitler is dead." As if the Führer couldn't possibly die, only Adolf Hitler. "Didn't you hear about it? It was on the radio. Dönitz is his successor—Grand Admiral Dönitz," he corrected himself. "You mustn't go out, not today. The British have imposed a round-the-clock curfew. The British are already in City Hall, City Commmandant General Wolz has surrendered the city without resistance. Without resistance, that means without honor," he said, staring at her out of his bulging blue eyes. "You can go on fighting in the underground resistance if you like, Mr. Lammers, as a *Werwolf,*" said Lena Brücker. "So now give me back my apartment key. We don't need an air-raid warden anymore." Lammers's lips twitched; a groan escaped that land-registry mouth, a moan, a whimper. Laboriously he extricated the key from the bunch. She walked up the stairs, hearing behind her: ideals, betrayal, Verdun, Fatherland, profiteers, and then barely intelligible, foreverfaithfulyessir!

At the top of the stairs she unlocked her front door. Bremer came out of the storeroom, pale, panic showing in his face, "I thought someone was coming, the block warden!" "Don't worry!" she said, "he's standing downstairs, making a long face for those fallen in battle."

"If we lose the war, we lose our honor," said Bremer. "Nonsense, to hell with honor," said Lena Brücker. "The war will soon be over. Dönitz is Hitler's successor."

"The Grand Admiral," said Bremer, now once again the boatswain with the Narvik shield and the Iron Cross Second Class. "That's good. Has Dönitz negotiated with the Americans? With the British? Are they finally turning against Russia?"

He was putting the answer right in her mouth. "Yes, I think so, yes," said Lena Brücker, and it wasn't that far from the truth, for through an intermediary Himmler had made the Allies an offer: separate peace with England and the United States in order to march jointly against Russia. "That's exactly what we need: jeeps, corned beef, and Camels."

"Of course," said Bremer, "Dönitz'll see to that." "Yes," she said, although at that point Dönitz, far from negotiating, was broadcasting rallying cries in every direction and ordering deserters shot. Bremer stared at the crossword puzzle. Winged horse: seven letters. Clear as day. He looked up: "At last," he said, "at last Churchill has woken up! Now," he said, getting to his feet, "we'll fight the Russians. A negotiated peace with the West, clear as day," he said again. She didn't understand. He had stood up, said, "Here," and laid the school atlas on the table. Only at this point did she realize that he had taken the atlas from the cupboard. So he must have searched—searched through storeroom, cupboards, chest, and bedside tables, for this atlas had lain in the cupboard drawer, right at the bottom, and on top of it the letters, a few from her son and, neatly tied those special ones from him, from Klaus, the button salesman. "Who's that?" I asked. "That," said Mrs. Brücker, "is another story. Nothing to do with curried sausage."

He must have read the letters, she thought, poked around and read everything. And I can't even ask him, a question like that is absurd, he would merely say No, just as he had lied to her when she had asked him whether he was married. The wallet with the photo had just been lying there; but in her absence he must have gone through all her things—that surely made a difference. And he didn't even try to explain how he came to be holding the atlas in his hand. He stood there, and she thought, he's standing there like so many men in uniform whose photos and pictures we've been shown these past years: the Führer, the commanders in chief of the army, or the navy, bent over maps spread out on map tables under reading lamps, or folded beneath a pointing gloved finger, or in army vehicles, small crumpled maps in trenches, lying in the mud. "Here's where they start their advance," he said. "The British, so the commanding admiral used to maintain, will lose this war even if they win it. Then it's curtains for the British Empire, then the Russians will have reached the North Sea. This is where they will advance, take back Berlin, then Breslau, then Königsberg, a pincer movement from above, gigantic, the Kurland pocket will be reinforced, our naval units will leave port, finally under the protection of fighter planes—besides, many vessels are still intact."

She had never seen him so animated, unfamiliar somehow, so enthusiastic, but suddenly he flopped down on the sofa, and—there was no other way to put it—his expression darkened, a cloud came up, a pitch-black cloud: Now he's thinking, she thought, that he'll be shut up in here, that he can't possibly get out, can't take part in the advance. Not that he'd have been a hero, he never saw himself as that, but still there's a difference between fighting when everything is moving forward, victories are being celebrated, special announcements: Tarantara. U-boats in the Atlantic, Lieutenant-Commander Kretschmer has sunk 100,000 gross registered tons of enemy units. Oak-leaves with swords. *Les Préludes* on the radio. Or being part of a retreat, in which case all that matters is to somehow get home and if possible, all in one piece.

"I see," he said, as he sat brooding and self-absorbed on the sagging sofa. "That's why we don't hear any more shooting."

She could imagine what he was thinking but not saying: that he was a deserter, that he would go on being cooped up in this apartment, that he might have to stay here for months, maybe years, that it wasn't inconceivable that Germany might win the war, which meant he would never be able to get out.

The open atlas lay there, suddenly ignored. On picking it up she saw that he had carefully drawn in the front lines as they were the day he deserted: In the north, Bremen had been captured, the British had crossed the Elbe at Lauenburg, the Americans had shaken hands with the Russians at Torgau. Not much left of the German Reich. Lammers from downstairs had said: "The Führer simply refused to listen to the stars. Surely it was obvious that, when Pluto and Mars were in conjunction, we should have fired the V2s at London, at Downing Street. The stars don't lie," said Lammers. "Roosevelt dies, he hated Germans, a Jew of course. Truman, on the other hand, saw things clearly. Churchill too, of course, though he drank too much, but he must have realized what they were all stumbling into. Communism, Bolshevism. Enemy of mankind." They were all talking about the turning point. Turning point, that was another of those Nazi phrases. The turning point is coming. Bremer the boatswain had said: "When the turning point comes, keep your head down."

There he sat, a shadow of apprehension on his face, a questioning line creasing his forehead, a bit crooked, a line that crept upward, a bit bent, still without contour.

"I sat down beside him on the sofa, and he put his head on my shoulder. Slowly his head slipped down onto my breast, and that's how I held him, thinking: If he starts to cry now, I'll tell him. I stroked his hair, that fine blond hair, cut short and parted on the right. And slowly, very slowly, his head slipped onto my lap, his hand moved in under my shirt, slowly pleading, once I had to get up briefly to free the material.

"Later, on the mattress island, he was listening. 'Strange,' he said, 'no alarm, no shooting. Uncanny, the silence. So sudden.' And he added something he had been told during his military training, a result of many years' experience of ground warfare: 'When there's silence, always be on your toes. Yesterday the British were shooting all day across the Elbe. Today this uncanny silence.'"

She interrupted her knitting to hold up part of the sweater: "Does the tree trunk look all right like that?"

Dark brown, almost black, the trunk that was eventually to become a fir tree rose from the light brown of the hills. The blue of a cloudless day in the valley was already visible.

"Can you see the horizon?"

"Yes," I replied.

"But now it gets difficult, with the branches of the fir tree."

"How do you manage that?"

"I used to knit a lot. Maybe a cat by a lantern, maybe a little sailboat. Once a balloon. By that time my eyesight had already almost gone. And over and over again, landscapes with hills, sun, and fir trees. Even with clouds—I could actually knit whole banks of clouds. But I don't think I could manage those anymore. How do you like this scene?"

"Very nice. Maybe another two or three rows of blue with the tree trunk."

"Good," she said, looking past me. She counted and began knitting again with a blue strand, carrying along a black strand that was to grow farther up into the sky.

"So the next day Bremer asked me to go down onto the street, at least for a moment. Couldn't I try and find a radio tube? I told him I already had—no luck."

But she did go downstairs, out onto the street, and once around the block. At Grossneumarkt, white sheets hung from those buildings that had not been destroyed. The British had issued orders for a round-the-clock curfew.

She walked up the stairs again.

On the fourth floor, squeezed into her own front door, Mrs. Eckleben was waiting.

"'See any Tommies?'"

"'Not a soul.'"

"'What are you up to at night anyway? The lamp in the kitchen wobbles, and the ceiling shakes.'"

"It was dark, of course, she couldn't see me blushing furiously. I told her I did my exercises.

"Upstairs Bremer was waiting. 'The streets are totally deserted—curfew.'

"'Let's wait,' he told me, 'better keep quiet, or someone will notice us—besides, it's nice here.'

"I was almost as tall as him, I used to be five foot ten, he didn't have to bend down—mouth to mouth, eye to eye, without my having to lift my head."

They lay on the mattress raft, under a quilt—there was no way the kitchen could be made piping hot long enough so one could lie there naked—and she told him about her husband, Gary, whose real name was Willi and who was a motor-launch skipper, used to carry dock workers across the Elbe, to Deutsche Werft and to Blohm und Voss. When the kids were in school in the mornings, she would go down to the pier, it wasn't far, and join him in the wheelhouse. Just go for a ride across the Elbe. The wind pushed up the waves. The launch pitched. The spray beat against the glass panes. He would put his arm around her and say: "Someday we'll just sail away, across the Atlantic, sail to America, find ourselves an island." That feeling: a tingling in one's stomach—waves, real waves, were something wonderful.

They had been married five years when Gary started making night trips. At first she thought nothing of it, but then that there might be a woman. The odd thing was that when he came home early in the morning he slept with her. "I'm on night shift," he'd say. Since he didn't own the launch he couldn't set his working hours. Made good money at that time. Night work meant double pay. They could buy themselves a few things: living-room furniture, cupboard, two armchairs, full-length mirror, and four chairs, all birchwood and polished. He bought himself suits, expensive ones. English cloth, top quality. And shoes. American shoes. The lord of the alleys, they called him in the neighborhood. This embarrassed her. He was out of keeping with the area. Walked around like some director, smoking cigars, Loeser & Wolf, genuine Havanas too. Sometimes he was woken up at night by the street-door bell. Someone would come and say: "Get a move on, you're needed." He would dress, hurriedly, and give her a kiss. And it would be morning before he came back. "Had to take some sailors to their ships," he would say. It was very strange. One night, when she was already asleep, his voice said: "Come on, Lena my girl, you have to come along. Hurry up and get dressed." On with her coat, her head scarf. Outside it was raining. No, not just raining, a storm was blowing. Down below a taxi waited. "The harbor, please, the piers." That's where his launch was tied up. The sidekick he normally took along hadn't shown up. Someone always had to be there to tie up when coming alongside. That night they went out onto the Elbe, the water was rough, the waves had whitecaps. And it was pitch-dark. It was dangerous, she could tell by the way he stood there, gripping the wheel, a cold cigarette between his lips. "What's up?" He didn't answer. He was too busy taking the waves at the right angle.

"A coastal vessel looms up out of the rain. Gary moves slowly toward it, almost alongside, heading for the harbor. A light signal from the vessel: three short, two long. Gary picks up the flashlight: four short, one long, steers closer to the other boat, behind the stern, we rock wildly. 'Now!' he shouts. 'Now catch the line!' They threw a line across. 'Secure it, belay it properly!' I know all the knots from my father, he used to work on lighters, so I secure it, I'm wet, wet from the rain, wet from the water with spray coming across, and Gary wrenches the wheel this way and that, the launch has to cut through the waves cleanly so it won't be swamped. And there are the stern waves from the ship too. And then, splash, they throw something overboard. The ship turns away. 'Hurry!' shouts Gary. I've always had plenty of guts, I pulled it toward me, it was yellow. Christ, Lena, I think, that's a person, hanging in a life jacket, pale face, it's a child, and I scream. 'What's wrong?' shouts Gary. 'Pull, dammit, pull! And hold on tight!' I keep pulling and pull the bundle out of the water. 'Hold on tight!' he shouts. I pull it aboard, something pale, a parcel, oilcloth, that's why it's so pale. I realized what it was that Gary was doing here: smuggling.

"'What *is* it?'" I asked when I stood next to him again in the wheelhouse. 'Nothing,' he said, 'you know nothing, you've seen nothing.' I was soaking wet and shivering. My teeth were chattering. He put his arm around me and he was whistling, in a good mood. And he didn't have to wrench the wheel as much anymore now that we were moving with the wind and the waves were coming from astern. Went then to the Old Harbor pub, where the parcel was handed over to some fellow, a stunted giant. We had a grog. And another. In the pub Gary played on his pocket comb. 'What would you like?' he asked. 'La Paloma,' I said. No one could play on the comb like he could. A little piece of tissue paper over it, and he could play 'The Internationale,' or 'Brothers, awaken to sunlight and freedom,' or any number of hit tunes. Could have gone on the vaudeville stage. Never learned to play a regular instrument. Only the comb. But that he did so well it made women feel weak in the knees.

"His escapades grew longer and longer. The lord of the alleys. He'd stay away for nights on end, then come home, crawl into the warm bed, and claim his pleasure. Lied. He'd say, 'It's nothing, truly,' and take me in his arms. And I believed him because I wanted to believe. But I knew it wouldn't help, not one bit, if I told him: I don't believe that. It's no use kidding oneself. Love is beautiful because you're a couple, but that's also the pain," said Mrs. Brücker, "that's why it's so difficult to separate. And most people manage it only when they have someone else they can be a couple with." She lay beside him, wide awake, and knew when he was deeply asleep, when he was dreaming, and when he was snoring. Nothing wrong with that. Oh well. But that night, after the stormy trip on the

Elbe, they walked home arm in arm and slightly tipsy from the grog, she in her wet clothes. "But I felt warm, from the inside, through and through. He was good at that.

"Two months later, one evening, he's sitting in the kitchen, drinking his beer and eating fried potatoes, when the doorbell rings, there stood the police. Took him along right away. He was sentenced to three years in jail but served only one. That was the end of his launch-skipper career. Luckily he also had a truck driver's license, so he took to driving, long distance. Skipper of the highway. To Denmark, Belgium, but mostly Dortmund and Cologne, where he had various women. Used to come home to pick up clean underwear. He was"—she hesitated, looked at me with her milky-blue eyes—"a heel. Yes," she said, "you might think I'm being unfair, no, he was a heel, but a heel who was a wizard at playing the comb."

That's how she told it to me, and that's how she must have also told it to Bremer the deserter as he lay beside her in the kitchen, on the mattresses, probably with only a hint of the dialect that was to become more marked in her old age, something I also happened to notice with my mother, in whose voice, as she grew older, you could hear more and more of the Hamburg dialect. And Bremer? Bremer lay there and listened. He was twenty-four and, apart from a few war experiences she didn't want to hear about, had nothing much to tell. "But just lying beside him like that was really wonderful, body to body. You can talk to each other that way too, without saying a word. My body had been deaf and dumb—for almost six years, with that one exception, New Year's Eve 1943." She told Bremer about that too. "For me it was wonderful to talk, about past times. He listened. He hadn't let on, had he, that he had a wife. And a baby. Maybe that was why he had nothing to say. I'd have taken him home and hidden him regardless. That had nothing to do with attraction. I'd have helped anybody who was ready to quit. Simply hid him. After all, it's the little things that trip the big fellows up. Just that there have to be a lot of us to really bring them down. Your grandmother now, she had guts. There was one time when she really went into action. D'you know the story about the truncheon?"

"No," I lied, so as to hear it again from Mrs. Brücker's lips. A story I had heard as a child more than once from my aunt, an incident that had occurred in the summer of 1943. My grandmother, a robust, gray-haired woman with a formidably corseted stomach, daughter of a Rostock baker, recipient of the Mother's Cross, had never been interested in politics.

She was busy raising five children. But later she did demonstrate against rearmament. She lived on Alter Steinweg, and because she was such a redoubtable woman they had made her an air-raid warden. After the first major air raid on Hamburg, in July '43, she had rescued two children from the flames, her hair had been singed, and all that was left of her eyelashes were tiny little yellow-brown knobbles. Russian prisoners of war were shoveling away the debris on Alter Steinweg: emaciated figures, their heads shaved. Latvian SS soldiers goaded them on with rubber truncheons. That's when my grandmother, her steel helmet hanging like a shopping basket over her arm, went up to a truncheon-wielding SS soldier and took away his truncheon, leaving the man flabbergasted. There were many witnesses. "That's enough," she had said. Then she simply continued on her way, and nobody dared touch her.

"A person must be able to say No," said Mrs. Brücker, "like Hugo. He has guts. Diapers the old folks in the nursing department. I've made a lot of mistakes. And often looked the other way. But then, at the very end, I had a chance. Maybe the best thing I ever did, hiding someone so he wouldn't be killed and couldn't kill others either. What happened later—that had to do with everything being over so quickly. D'you see?"

No, I didn't, but I said Yes so she would go on with her story.

They lay in the kitchen on the mattress island and listened. How silent it was. Once they heard a car with a loudspeaker. A voice, squawking and distorted, some distance away. "Listen," he said. "Can you make anything out? What's he saying? Is it German?" She listened. "It's just nonsense." She began telling him about blackout practice during the first few days of the war, at that time, too, there was always someone driving around in a car with a loudspeaker. "They'll be doing it now because of the Russians, who also have planes, but pretty lame ducks, so I've heard." "Shut up," he said, "be quiet, can't you? Damn it all!" and for a moment he got really furious, but she went on talking, persistently, frantically loud. He jumped up and ran to the window. "Watch out!" she called after him. "Don't open the window!" The loudspeaker fell silent. "Sounded like English to me," he said. "Forget it, that was a fellow with some kind of dockside dialect, the district chief, I know him. Name of Frenssen." She raised the quilt, but he didn't want to lie down again. He put on his pea jacket and went over to the window. There he stood with his bare thin legs, staring down.

A distant, profound silence. From time to time bombers flew over the city. No detonations. She had fallen asleep. She smacked her lips in her sleep. He lay down again. Once during the night the sirens wailed briefly, as if the city were sighing in a nightmare filled with burning trees, liquid asphalt, and screaming torches.

He had served way up north on his patrol boat until, thanks to his equestrian badge, he was transferred. Riding was something he enjoyed. He had only to stroke a sweating horse's rump and then sniff his hand: that smell of air, horse sweat, and leather clinging to his hand would remind him of Petershagen, of the Weser River, where the meadows reached right down to the water's edge, the river swirling along the banks, not fast but still with a visible current and many little eddies.

In the morning he woke up, heard voices from the street. Even a car from the cross-street, not one of those charcoal-burning affairs, a different sound, quieter than a diesel. "There are people out on the street," he said from the window. "The curfew has been lifted." Wouldn't she please go down, right away, to have a look? At once. He urged her as if he couldn't wait to get out of the kitchen, out of the apartment. He didn't even allow her time to make coffee, no hug. He stood there fully dressed, as if anxious to get going, out, dash off—that's how he was looking down on Brüderstrasse.

She walked to Grossneumarkt. People were standing around talking about the British, who had occupied the city since the day before. The city had been transferred from a commanding general in a gray uniform to a different one in khaki. There had been some looting, but no women had been molested. For sure, no chocolate had been handed out to the kids. As always, lineups had formed at the hydrants. However: There were no more German uniforms to be seen, no gray ones, no navy blue, let alone brown. She walked toward Rathausmarkt. On Michaelis Bridge she saw her first British soldier. He was perched on an armored reconnaissance car, wearing a beret, with leather patches on the shoulders of his sweater. Somehow that sweater reminded her of a chain-mail tunic. He wore loose khaki pants, gaiters, laced boots. Inside the reconnaissance car was another Tommy, wearing a headset and speaking into a radio transmitter. The man on the top of the car had turned his face to the sun. So those are the conquerors, sitting there soaking up the sun, she thought. Alongside the reconnaissance car there was a group of German soldiers, squatting on the curb. One of them had a little cart loaded with a rucksack and two field packs, the kind the Reichswehr used to have, covered in calfskin. The men were middle-aged. Their equipment randomly thrown together. One of them, an elderly man with a plaster on his nose, had a wool blanket slung around his shoulders like a big sausage. They looked unshaven and weary. The British soldier ignored the Germans, and the Germans ignored him. Only the Germans didn't turn their faces to the sun. Most of them sat there staring into space. One of them had pulled off a boot, laid the sock, which was full of holes, on the ground, and was picking at the skin between his toes. Now and then he sniffed his finger.

On returning to Brüderstrasse she saw a crowd outside her building. Neighbors had gathered there, and strangers, also two German policemen. And her first thought was: Bremer's being arrested. Maybe someone had discovered him, or maybe on his own he had risked leaving the apartment and found out from Mrs. Eckleben that the war was over.

Lena Brücker pushed her way through the people crowding the stairwell. Mrs. Claussen was among them, and my Aunt Hilde, who lived downstairs on the second floor and in whose kitchen I had loved to sit as a child. "Poor man," said Mrs. Eckleben, "he couldn't bear the disgrace." "What is it?" asked Lena Brücker, "who is it, for God's sake?", her heart feeling like an icy stone. Aunt Hilde pointed to the entrance to Lammers's apartment on the ground floor, where Eisenhart the watchmaker was later to move in. A man was trying to catch Lammers's jackdaw: it had escaped from its open cage and was fluttering in panic around the room. "Where's Lammers?" Mrs. Eckleben pointed to the corridor where, in the dark, outside the door to the air-raid cellar, Lammers was hanging from a rope knotted to the banister above. He was wearing his block warden's uniform, and his head lolled to one side, as if he wanted to lean against something, a shoulder or a breast. He must have put on his big steel helmet from the first war, for it had fallen off his head and was now lying under him like a pisspot.

Upstairs she unlocked her apartment door, and just as she was wondering whether she shouldn't tell him now that the war was over, at least in Hamburg, and that in the stairwell Lammers was hanging from a rope, Bremer asked: "Are the British here?" "Yes," she replied, "I saw them, they're on Michaelis Bridge, with some German soldiers. Soaking up the sunshine."

"You see!" he said. "I knew it, the time has come, now they'll move against the Russians."

"Yes," she said, "maybe. A newspaper? There aren't any yet, news is announced over loudspeakers and on the radio. The Dönitz government has called upon the population to maintain discipline, nobody's allowed to leave their post." He took her in his arms. "The stores are to open again. The authorities are to resume work. Tomorrow I'll be going back to work." She kissed him.

"What about me?" he asked. "What am I supposed to do?"

"Wait, for the time being."

5

IT WAS THE FOURTH AFTERNOON,
and Mrs. Brücker said she wanted to go out.

"It's raining, and there's practically a gale blowing," I said.

"That's exactly why. I love walking around in the
rain, and I don't like to ask Hugo—that boy has
enough on his hands, he can do without getting wet as
well. D'you know what a tribe of South Sea Islanders
do with their old people? They bend down a palm
tree, and the old woman must hang on to it, then they
cut the rope and whoosh, up she goes. If the old
woman still has enough strength to cling on, that's
fine, then she can climb down the tree again. But
when she can't hang on, up she goes up to Heaven.
Nice, don't you agree?"

I asked her where she would like me to drive
her.

"To the Dammtor station, if you don't mind."
This was where she had stood as a child, with her
schoolmates, to welcome the Kaiser, who always got
off the train at Dammtor when he came to Hamburg.
"Hail to the conqueror!" the class had sung, but she,

to the same tune, sang: "Fried potatoes with herring tail!" Her father was a socialist and a member of the union, a man with an impressive bald pate.

She had me bring her raincoat from the cupboard, a dark-green mackintosh, at least fifty years old. She covered her brimless brown hat with a plastic rain-bonnet that tied under the chin with two tapes, doing all this with calm, tentative movements. "Right," she said, "off we go now."

I drew up outside the station, helped her out of the car, and told her she would have to wait a moment. It was a while before I found a parking spot, and even then it was some way off. I ran back to the station, thinking she might have become impatient, walked off, and lost her way in the general hubbub. I had a vision of a crowd gathering around Mrs. Brücker as if she were a lost child. But there she was, in her bottle-green mackintosh, standing just where I had dropped her off, holding on to the railing like on a boat, and tilting her face toward the gusts of rain as if on the lookout. She insisted on walking through the railway underpass, where the rear windows of the station kitchen used to be, then she had me lead her past the villa on Dammtorstrasse, the former site of a police station, and finally she wanted to go on to the war memorial of the 76th regiment. A big block of sandstone with a company of life-size soldiers marching around it: "Germany must live, even if we must die."

"That gives you a thrill, doesn't it," she said.

I described the condition of the monument, which had been sprayed by pacifists with red and black paint. The faces of some of the soldiers had been chiseled away. A protest.

"I get it," she said. "But two of the soldiers have pipes in their mouths. I always showed those to my kids. The others all look alike." I walked around the monument with her, looking for the soldiers with pipes. Their faces had not been damaged.

"That's good," she said.

She was ready to go home. We walked slowly back to the main entrance of the station, without speaking, she clinging to my arm. I believe she wanted to feel the rain in her face, wanted to hear the sounds of the city from close up: in the underpass the rumble of the train wheels, cars starting up, scraps of conversation, hurried footsteps, loudspeaker announcements. I imagine she wanted to walk past a place that had a special significance in her life. I didn't dare ask her.

At the station entrance I asked her to wait again, brought back the car, stopped, jumped out, pulled her over to the car, aggressive honking behind us. "We have to hurry," I said, helping, no, pushing her into the seat, exasperated by the honking of those impatient idiots. She didn't say anything, but I could see she had hurt herself, strained her back. I drove her home. She said she was exhausted, she couldn't tell me anything more today. Nor tomorrow either.

That was the day we exchanged only a few sentences. Yet as we were walking through the rain, the light pressure on my arm made me clearly aware of the strength this woman had needed to live her life and preserve her dignity.

I didn't drive across to Harburg to see her again until two days later.

In the meantime I had telephoned a friend, an Englishman, an ethnologist and avid traveler. I had asked him about curry, food for the gods. "Nonsense. Curry for an Indian, the way you get it in cans—it's on a par with McDonald's. Curry comes from the Tamil word *kari*, which means roughly sauce or gravy. Varying amounts of spices are added to the food according to taste, an art of blending to suit the individual. With sixteen or even twenty different spices, there are almost limitless flavor variations. A cure for depression? Yes," said Ted, a convinced rationalist, "quite possibly. Chili, for example, speeds up the circulation, thus enhancing the sense of well-being. Ginger and cardamon are said to be antidepressants and aphrodisiacs. That laughing dream, if the curry had been a good blend, is not unlikely." Once after eating curry he had dreamed he was a civet cat, endowed with a fabulous scent gland. When he woke up he had to take refuge outdoors.

I had also gone to the Hamburg State Library and asked for the microfilms of the last editions of the *Hamburger Zeitung* up to May 2 and the first edition of May 7. I could hardly believe it, but the librarian assured me that it was the same journalists who one week were still writing about final victory and fighting to the last man, and the next week were expounding the decrees of the British city commandant. Yet in those few days something had changed. Words had regained a little of what they really meant. They no longer distorted reality as they had before. "Obviously," said the librarian, "he who pays the piper calls the tune." All such terms as defensive battles, miracle weapons, home front, had disappeared; and even the "wild vegetables," which as late as May 1 had still been extolled as being particularly tasty so as to make the shortages more acceptable, were now—one week after the surrender—called nettles and young dandelions. True, the recipes remained the same. But of course it does make a difference whether you eat wild vegetables or dandelion leaves, which latter promptly bring rabbits to mind.

"Life went on. Somehow," said Mrs. Brücker. "It was really nice to know that, when you got home, someone was waiting for you and had even tidied up the place. Bremer made everything shipshape, just like he had learned in the navy. But then he had nothing else to do. The kitchen had never been as spick and span as while Bremer was living up there." The saucepans were nested according to size, the handles one above the other and all facing the same way. Bowls arranged according to size. Pans not only washed but scoured with sand. The chopping boards lay stacked like roof tiles on the counter; the knives, sharpened, glinted on the wall. And even the oven, which she hadn't cleaned for years, was so spotless that a year later she was still almost reluctant to slide in her first roast. When she came home, Bremer would be standing in the corridor. He would put his arms around her, and they would kiss, but day by day the kisses became more perfunctory—she could feel the inner tension in his back as he stood there stiff as a poker. He couldn't wait to ask what was going on outside, whether there were any newspapers, whether she had found a radio tube, where the front line might be that day. So she had to make a report. In doing so she didn't have to tell many lies, since at first nothing much changed.

Two British officers had turned up at the food

office, a captain and a major. Both spoke German with a Hamburg accent. They began by examining the personal dossiers of the executives. Then Lena Brücker was questioned. "You are in charge of the canteen?" "Yes, but only as a substitute." "Were you a party member?" "No." "Any other party affiliations?" "No." The captain wanted to know which of the executives had been in the SA or SS. Whereupon Lena Brücker said: "You'd better ask them. You can see right away who's lying." The officer understood, laughed, and said: "Okay!"

The jeep, corned beef, and the German soldier—simply unbeatable. So Dr. Fröhlich had said. Fröhlich spoke after the British major, who had briefly informed them that supplies for the population must be secured, so for the time being they must all remain at their work posts. Then came Dr. Fröhlich, speaking not in his brown party uniform, not in breeches and high boots, but in a plain gray suit; instead of a party badge on his label, a small Hamburg coat of arms.

Dr. Fröhlich spoke of the mess that had been made—"Who by?" Lena Brücker asked Holzinger, who was sitting beside her. "By the brown jokers, who else?" Fröhlich spoke about the joint efforts needed to clean up this mess—"What a shit he is," said Lena Brücker, this time a little louder. Fröhlich cried,

"Let's go!" and again, "Let's go! Now we have to work until"—at that point Lena Brücker could stand it no longer, loud and clear she burst out with "until final victory!"—"final victory!" he cried. He hesitated: "Did I say final victory? No, a new beginning, of course, and reconstruction!" Then, as he had been taught to say as a little boy in Bavaria, "*Grüss Gott*," but when he wanted to shake hands with the British major—who was, after all, as Fröhlich would not long ago have put it, a member of the Kike clan—the major simply ignored the hand, leaving Fröhlich standing there for a moment, awkward and annoyed, before he turned on his heel and left the room without a word. But he didn't leave his post as administrator of the food office—at least not right now; for the time being he was indispensable, that competent administrator with his legal background. It was four weeks before he was replaced and sent to an internment camp for nine months. Then he returned to the food office and was demoted to personnel manager. One of the first steps he took was to fire Lena Brücker.

"But we're not that far yet," said Mrs. Brücker. She held up the half-finished sweater. The green fir tree was already spreading its branches into the blue of the sky. Now began the section that required frequent interruptions on her part, counting, fingering. . . . Meanwhile I was roped in to tell her when the next branch was due. She was now working with three strands: blue for the sky, green for the tree, and a light brown that yielded a final hilltop reaching high up into the blue. "That was the only time I ever spoke up at a public meeting," she said. "In those days Holzinger was already saying, 'The Nazis won't stop growing, just like a corpse's fingernails.'"

Holzinger stayed on as head chef of the canteen. After the British officers tasted the goulash soup he had prepared for them, he wasn't even asked whether he had been a party member.

The major had left Hamburg in 1933. At that time he had been able to take his library with him. The captain had fled shortly before the outbreak of war, taking along only a briefcase that contained shaving kit, pajamas, a photograph of his parents, and his passport stamped with the J. "They looked very smart in their khaki uniforms with those big side-pockets. They had much less leather on their bodies than German soldiers, who always smelled like sweating horses," said the odor-sensitive Mrs. Brücker. The captain had offered Lena Brücker a cigarette, and she had taken one. When he offered to light it for her, she told him that, if he didn't mind, she'd rather smoke it after work. "He always gave me such a look—well, I don't know how to describe it, he'd have liked to fraternize with me, something that at the time was still forbidden to the British." After that, Captain Friedländer used to offer two, sometimes three cigarettes a day, and Bremer would smoke them in the evening. One before supper, one after supper, and one after they had been adrift on the mattress raft.

"Bremer would light a cigarette, a Players, and inhale so that the smoke would disappear way down inside him and then a moment later reappear in little clouds. Goodness gracious, people who produce cigarettes like that also win wars!"

Bremer had sharpened pencils, red, green, yellow, and brown, the atlas lay on the table. Important briefing at the admiral's headquarters. Bremer had drawn in the positions of the British, Germans and Americans and now wanted to know what points the troops had reached according to the latest reports. She had heard in the canteen that Montgomery was continuing his advance toward the east, to meet the Red Army, while Eisenhower had ordered his troops to stop at the Elbe. So: Wismar, Magdeburg, Torgau.

Lena Brücker had avoided the word surrender in connection with the city of Hamburg, that was all. What happened then needed only a few key words to guide Bremer's imagination in the direction in which the secret or openly expressed wishes of many people were moving: That just before total defeat the tide might turn. When Roosevelt died, Hitler wasn't the only one hoping for a new Russian about-face, another miracle like the one they handed Frederick the Great. Jointly with the Americans and Tommies against Ivan. The Germany army. Hardened in icy winters, on muddy runways, on dry steppes. Maybe the war wasn't quite lost after all, maybe they could finagle their way out of disaster—and that also meant: out of guilt.

"There was something touching," she said, "about the way he sat there when I came home in the evening from work. It always made me think of my Jürgen, and I'd say to myself, I hope the boy's all right. Just that Jürgen was sixteen and Bremer was twenty-four, after all. On the other hand, I was the one who invented the front line he proceeded to pencil in. He would then imagine further objectives of the advances, toward Berlin of course, and Breslau, the surrounded city that was still being defended, heroically. 'So things are going well,' he'd say, but then suddenly he'd frown, and his expression would become puzzled, or rather, anxious. You see, the more successful the troops were, and the farther east they advanced, the longer the war would drag on, and that meant the longer he would be cooped up in that apartment, for weeks, months, or—he broke out in a sweat—years. Of course he wanted the war to end, as quickly as possible and, if possible, in victory too. But even then, supposing there was a peace treaty, he was caught there, and now it occurred to him for the first time that he had fallen into a woman's trap. Voluntarily, to be sure, but, as it now turned out, a trap all the same."

If he was honest with himself, it hadn't been just fear of the tanks or of the British: he had stayed because on that cold rainy morning, lying beside Lena, his hand on the pillow of her warm soft breasts, the idea of getting up in order to clamber into a wet cold hole in the ground for the purpose of getting killed had seemed so utterly wrongheaded, perverse even. And at that moment she had said: "You can stay." If he had hidden somewhere in a barn or an empty toolshed and the British had approached, he would have come out and surrendered, told the British military police—who would, of course, be working with the German MPs—that he had lost contact with his unit. There was so much confusion in those days that his case wouldn't have attracted much attention. At worst he could have expected a dressing down, but now: the firing squad.

This feeling of being trapped made him pace up and down the apartment during the day like a caged animal; made him, after he had finished up in the kitchen, having washed the dishes, cleaned, wiped, polished, scrubbed, constantly return to the window and look down on the street, go into the living room, from the living room to the bedroom, from there back to the kitchen, do a bit of the crossword puzzle, then back again to the window.

"There was a constant slight vibration of the ceiling, a faint squeaking," Mrs. Eckleben, who used to live under Mrs. Brücker, tells me. "It wasn't that loud, not loud enough to hear footsteps, but you could hear, I mean sense, quite distinctly, that there was someone up there."

I am sitting in an apartment in which the furniture is Scandinavian, pale shades of blue and gray, a beige rug. Mrs. Eckleben's daughter is a teacher and close to retirement. For my visit she has made coffee and brought out her homemade plum torte. I accepted a big dollop of whipped cream. Mrs. Eckleben had once been employed in the telegraph office of the German Reich Post Office. She emphasizes that she takes a cold shower every morning, and she is proud of her accurate memory, which is in fact amazingly good. Physically, too, she is in fine shape and goes for a two-hour walk through Sasel very day. Each time she raises her coffee cup to her lips, she sticks out her little finger. She talks about the war years. At one point she gets up, tells her daughter, who also jumps up, "Don't bother, Grete, you have a bad back, I can manage," and goes to the cupboard, bends down, opens a drawer, and takes out a photo album. She shows me what she looked like as a young woman, as she says. She was forty at that time. "That's my husband, Georg, killed at Smolensk, he was an artillery sergeant. A little more coffee?" "Yes, please." Neither she nor Mrs. Brücker know that I know: It wasn't Lammers who reported to the Gestapo, it was she, Mrs. Eckleben. I have read the reports in the archives, read her statement concerning a young man called Wehrs. As a result, Wehrs was arrested and interrogated, in other words tortured:

"W. had the following to say about the Führer: A man who agitates for war in order to do business with Thyssen and Krupp. Armaments make politics; the little man has to stick his neck out. April 23, 1935."

"W. makes out-and-out speeches in our downstairs lobby: The National Socialist Party was a party of criminals. Horst Wessel was a failed student and a pimp. The Nazi bigwigs, especially Fatso Hermann [some Gestapo wit had written in the margin: The Supreme Commander of the Luftwaffe], are scoundrels, bums who live high on the hog. Gamblers, swindlers, morphine addicts, criminals. July 6, 1936."

That must have been shortly before his arrest. I also found an entry on Lena Brücker. The following are entries concerning morale listed by buildings and apartment numbers:

"L. Brücker does not agitate openly but often makes critical remarks that are bad for morale. For example, re the fuel supply situation. B: I don't think the Führer has such cold feet as I do. (General laughter.) Or: The Jews are human beings too. Or: The people love the Führer. That's more than I can take. I love my children. And used to love my husband. I know where this will get us. February 15, 1943."

A Gestapo entry on Lammers:

"Convinced National Socialist. But refuses to report on his neighbors. Unsuitable!"

To my regret, what he was unsuitable for is not mentioned. Perhaps one could find that out, too. I began turning pages, asking for files, but then I sent them back unread. Those tattered, yellowed pages would be another story. All I wanted to find out was how curried sausage was invented.

"A little more coffee?"

"No, thank you."

"The Brücker woman had hidden a man up there. At first I thought it was a deserter, possibly her son, he was an air-defense helper, you know. But then, after the surrender, I thought, maybe it's someone from the party or one of the SS, seeing how those boys were hounded after the defeat. They had all been idealists, after all. They were sent to Lorraine to the coal mines. Although," she goes on, "I wouldn't have thought the Brücker woman capable of hiding someone like that, considering her general attitude."

I could have explained to old Mrs. Brücker why Mrs. Eckleben suddenly started greeting her so cordially on the stairs. Lena Brücker couldn't figure it out. With a conspiratorial wink, Mrs. Eckleben pressed a pack of Overstolz cigarettes on her. "You're smoking again, I see!" said Mrs. Eckleben. And winked again.

Upstairs Bremer was waiting for her, didn't hug her, didn't kiss her, but asked: "D'you have a newspaper?"

"No, I don't. Instructions are given over the radio, so is the news. And the news is also displayed at the Gänsemarkt in the *Hamburger Zeitung* showcases." "So what's the latest?" "The Dönitz government is negotiating with the British about restoring train service between Hamburg and Flensburg. The usual stuff." "What's happened to all the paper?" "The largest newsprint stocks in North Germany are in flames." "How come?" "Arson." This is what she had read in the newspaper: A small stock of paper had burned up. Whether by spontaneous combustion or arson hadn't yet been determined.

"Arson," said Bremer, "must've been the SS."

"How do you know that?"

"It's obvious," he said, "of course, the SS. There will be conflicts between the SS and the navy, as well as the Wehrmacht, it's obvious, quite obvious. Dönitz will take care of them. The navy did its duty, wasn't involved in any dirty business, neither the attempt on the Führer's life nor any shooting of Russian prisoners of war."

"By the way," said Lena Brücker, "there won't be any more air raids, the Russians can't come all the way here with their bombers. Lammers has been relieved of his job as air-raid warden. He's left town. I wonder where he is now? I made him give me back my key, so no one's going to come in here. But you have to go on being quiet, walk around in your socks. In two weeks there'll be paper from America. It's already on the way. On Liberty ships." That was the time she had given herself, another two weeks; then she intended to tell him the truth.

One Saturday afternoon Lena Brücker came home from work and placed a plastic-wrapped, heat-sealed package on the table. "What is it?" Bremer asked, turning it over and over in his hands. Waterproof. Visible were small packets, crackers, candies, cans. "Iron rations," she said. "From old American army stocks." They had been distributed to an old age home and an orphanage. The captain had given this one to Lena.

"These packages," Lena Brücker told Bremer, "are being dropped on Russian positions. Propaganda. Instead of leaflets the Americans are dropping packages like this. They float down on little parachutes, nectar and ambrosia." With a knife, Bremer carefully slit open the plastic bag. How practical that was, sealed airtight, couldn't get wet or dry out: the salty crackers, not bad, fruit-drink crystals, a small can of honey, a can of cheese, a small can of sausage, a roll of hard candy. Four sticks of chewing gum.

He opened up one of the foil-wrapped sticks, broke it in two, and gave Lena half. For the first time in his life he put some chewing gum in his mouth. Thin and flat like cardboard; when chewed it crumbled into a mass which then slowly began to cohere and, mixed with saliva, became homogenous. They sat at the table and chewed. Looked at each other, watched each other's lower jaw move from side to side, a chewing that made them conscious of their teeth, a chewing that hardened their muscles, a chewing that produced a flavor, how should she describe it, could be anything. They looked at each other as they chewed, then burst out laughing. "What does your gum taste of?" He chewed and chewed. What was he to say? He felt as if he were in a trap: What does it taste of? Nothing, nothing, he would have had to say, nothing. Should he say strawberries? Cinnamon? Finally he uttered a long-drawn-out "We-ell." "Mine," she said, "tastes like toothpaste, mint." "Yes," he said, "you're right, peppermint, but it must be pretty old. I can taste only a hint of it." No, to be honest, he couldn't taste anything.

She opened the window. A breeze forced warmth into the kitchen. The sun was reflected in the windows across the street. It was dazzlingly bright. She undressed, without embarrassment, down to her bare skin, something she had never done before, and she did it although she was no longer twenty. She lay down beside him on the mattress raft. Lying propped on their elbows, they drank a few glasses of pear brandy and nibbled on the salty crackers. She wanted to turn on her other side, the left. Her right shoulder hurt, her back too, the side on which she had lugged home the bag of potatoes filched from the canteen. "Where does it hurt?" "Here," she said, touching her spine at the level of her pelvis. "I hope it isn't lumbago."

"Lie down," he said, "on your stomach. Easy now! Relax your fanny! Still tense! Relax completely!" Kneeling over her he began to massage her shoulder blades, then her spine, all the way down to her pelvis. Where had he learned that, she asked, those delicate yet firm movements? Looking after horses—his father was a veterinarian, hadn't he told her? She laughed so hard she got hiccups. So she had to hold her breath and count to twenty-one while he moved down her spine and with the knuckles of his first and second fingers kneaded the hollows between the vertebrae, delicately yet firmly, as far as her hips, when he shifted to the two dimples, working his thumbs into them in circles until the hairs on her neck stood deliciously on end, until she got hiccups again. "There's only one thing to do," he said, "arch your back, now press the small of your back forward, head down, legs slightly apart, relax, completely relax, raise your fanny, higher still, that's fine. And now take a deep breath. Relax! Breathe out! That's the way. Huhh!"

"It's a fact, it helps," said Mrs. Brücker and grinned, clacking her dentures.

The following Monday evening, Bremer said to Lena Brücker: "People on the street are walking faster." "Faster?" "Yes, a bit, just a little, but they are walking faster. Strange."

"No, quite simple," she said. "Things are picking up. People know where they're going."

And something else had struck him: a few women and men were standing on the street, singly, addressing passersby, the way hookers and pimps do, except that they were mostly elderly men and some shabbily dressed housewives. The next day he saw an amputee standing at the corner of Grosser Trampgang, the stump of his right leg resting on the hand-grip of his crutch; he was wearing a uniform, dyed a horrible shade of greenish brown, that looked like an off-color forestry uniform. Perhaps the man really had been taken on by the forestry service. Desk job. From time to time he raised his hand and showed three fingers as if wanting to play dice or display what he lacked. But what he lacked was a leg. Was he trying to indicate the number of his injuries? Bremer went for the launch-skipper's binoculars and looked down. No doubt about it, the man was addressing passersby. But they weren't merely passing by, they were hurrying by.

And then—it must have been the day after that—Bremer noticed a man who, despite the warm, in fact hot sun, was wearing a heavy winter coat. The man stood there in his voluminous dark-brown overcoat,

opening it for passersby, just briefly, like an exhibi-
tionist. Bremer was reminded of the French hookers
in Brest, in the winter of 1941, who would briefly open
their fur coats for him, like parting a curtain, to reveal
their red frilly garters, silk stockings, and black or red
push-up bras. Bremer stared down through the binoculars at the back of this balding man who at that
moment, opening his coat, turned toward a woman.
She looked, even asked him something, then shook
her head and walked on. Finally the man turned
around, opened his coat again, and Bremer got a
shock: he saw naked pink meat and a row of tits. The
man had half a pig tied to his body. Black market,
flashed through Bremer's mind, and suddenly he also
understood the amputee's finger movements. There
was no gambling here, no displaying of the number of
injuries; this was barter, and what was being shown
was the number of cigarettes to be exchanged for
other merchandise.

That evening he met Lena Brücker with the
words: "A black market has started up in front of this
building." And while she was heating up Holzinger's
barley soup, Bremer vented his annoyance at the col-
lapse of order and discipline out there. "What's so
bad about it?" asked Lena as she stood at the stove.
"All through the war years under-the-counter busi-

ness was being carried on the whole time. There's always been a black market, we know that." "But not so openly, not so blatantly, right out on the street. Down there is a man who's lost a leg, and he's trying to swap his silver wounds decoration."

In Bremer's mind, the German army, which a week ago had unconditionally surrendered, was standing at the gates of Berlin jointly with its American and British allies. Under the command of General Hoth, the right wing, reinforced by Americans, had just reached Görlitz, which meant, the Oder River. "It's really something," said Bremer, "the speed of it! The Russians have been bled white, they're finished, but all that is no excuse for the black market down there outside this building."

Bremer was sitting at the table eating the barley soup, which Lena Brücker had garnished with some chopped chervil. But he was eating as if without pleasure, spooning the soup into his mouth with a persistent, stolid greed that reminded her of her bald-headed father. "Don't you like the soup?" "Oh, I do!"

"Does it need more salt?" "No, no," said Bremer. But that double negative sounded as if he didn't care whether there were more salt or less in the soup. "They'll cross the Oder at Görlitz and then march on Breslau."

"It was a good time—to be exact, the best," she said, looping the blue strand of sky over her left forefinger: "If it hadn't been for all those stupid questions about troop movements. I was never interested in the war, nor in anything military, never liked uniforms, and now here was someone in my home fighting battles, and I had to keep thinking up new names, towns, you see—it was just crazy, and the worst part was that I had helped set the whole thing in motion. The reconquest of the east, what rubbish. Sometimes I wondered if I shouldn't simply have the newsprint arrive earlier, that would have put an end to the war, but also to Bremer and me."

"And did you speed it up?"

"No. That's the point—I didn't."

"Wasn't that unfair?"

"You know, the only unfair thing is old age. No. It was good. That was all. As simple as that. You lie there together, and you know that, when he gets up and leaves, all you have left is fifty- and sixty-year-old men. And they in turn dream only of younger women. That's the strange thing, for a long time getting old is something that happens only to other people. And then one day, somewhere around forty, you find it's happening to yourself: you notice a fine blue spidery mark, like a blue fireworks rocket: a little vein has burst on the inner side of your leg. And on your neck, here under your chin, between your breasts, you have creases, not many, just a few, especially in the morning, and looking at yourself you know you're getting old. But with Bremer I forgot all that. Yes," she said, "taken all around it was a good time, everything was a bit cockeyed, but that in itself was good too. Till it came to this row we had."

Exactly seventeen days after the surrender she came home and, without so much as a hello, he asked her right off: "D'you have a paper?"

"No."

"Why not? That's impossible! There must be newspapers. At least one sheet."

"No idea." And that slipped out rather brusquely. She'd had enough, nine hours' work, a half-hour walk to get there and half an hour back, no one had offered her a ride. And then the new doorman—a former police commissioner who had lost his job because he'd been a member of the Nazi party—had wanted to inspect her shopping bag. It contained a mess tin of turnip soup. It was only because of the British captain, who happended to be leaving the office at the same time and had said "Bye-bye!" to her, that she got away with it. That had been a scare at the end of the day. On her way home she had wondered whether she should tell him that the Americans needed the paper because they were dropping leaflets by the ton over the Russian positions. A simple comparison: how the American GI and the Russian soldier are fed each day—in the Cyrillic alphabet, of course. But that evening she didn't feel like concocting a story that must also hold water, because he would ask questions and want to know details. What leaflets, why aren't the British sending any paper? He insisted on knowing what exactly was going on, would she please get hold of a radio for him for a day? Just for one day, borrow it from someplace, maybe from one of her friends? When she told him that was impossible— what else could she say?—he became abusive. "You don't seem to want to—no, not *seem*, you just *don't* want to!" "I can't." "Yes you can! You just don't want to!" "No!" "Yes! *Why* can't you?" "Can't be done!" "You don't want to! I'm cooped up here." "So what?" "I stare down at the street. I clean up. I walk around in socks." By this time he was shouting. "Can't you understand? My life is on the line!" "Yes, okay," she said.

He was stunned, looked at her aghast for a moment. How did that word enter her head? His life is at stake, and she says okay. She suddenly felt sorry for him as he stood there crimson in the face, like a stubborn child. It was no longer a matter of life or death for him; it hadn't been for days. And because she felt sorry for him, she did exactly the wrong thing: "It's not as bad as you think," she said. Now he began to roar, and the more often she said "Sshh" the louder he roared. "The neighbors!" "I don't give a shit!" "What?" "They can kiss my ass. You're free to go wherever you like, but me? The MPs are waiting outside for me." "Nonsense." "Nonsense, you say? They'll put me up against a wall! And all you can say in nonsense, you say okay!" He swept his arm across the table, clearing everything off it—atlas, plates, cups, knives and forks, and glasses that shattered on the floor. He dashed to the door which, as always, she had automatically locked. He wanted out, and since she had removed the key—it had never occurred to her till then that she removed the key as if to keep him prisoner—he beat his fist, beside himself with rage, against the door handle, again and again, with all his might.

She put her arms around him from behind, wanting to calm him, to reassure him, but he went on hammering away at the door handle, so she tried to restrain him. That made him strike out behind, at her, so she pressed his arms as tightly as she could against his body: suddenly they were standing there wrestling with each other, she clinging to him from behind, he trying to free himself, to free his arms. They swayed, groaned, grunted, all without saying a word, drawing on every last ounce of their strength. He tried to twist his right arm out of her grip, in vain. She, who even as a girl had been capable of moving a lighter with a barge pole, pressed his arms against his body, pressed with all her strength. He dropped to the floor and, since she wouldn't let go, pulled her down with him. He rolled on to his back, his side, trying to force her away, swung around on to his stomach, scratching his face on the rough coconut runner as he whipped his head around and up. Now she felt the pressure of his arms slacken; no more jerking and straining. He dropped his head on the floor as if wanting to sleep. She let go of him, and he heaved a great sigh, a slowly subsiding gasp. He mumbled an apology and sat up. She pulled him to his feet by his left hand, the right one was bleeding, the knuckles, the skin had split open and was badly scraped. Only now did he feel pain, terrible pain. He held his hand under running cold water to prevent any further swelling. "Try moving your fingers," she said. He did, and it hurt, but he could move them. "So nothing's broken," she said.

For a moment she struggled with herself as to whether she should confess that she had been keeping something from him, in fact that she had lied to him, but now she could no longer say it, now it was too late.

It had been a game. Now it had turned serious, bloodily serious. To him it would now appear as a lowdown, dirty lie, as if she had meant to trick him, keep him like a household pet, make a fool of him, and finally drive him to a total loss of self-control. And hadn't she done exactly that? If she had at least let him twist her arm or strike her—she had never thought of that, instead she had held him in a grip of iron, using all her strength: in fact, she had defended herself. If she were now to sit across from him with a swollen eye and bruises on her arm, it would have made everything easier; she could have said, I just wanted to keep you here a bit longer. But now he was sitting there with his bandaged right hand, apologizing for having gone out of his mind.

They lay on the mattresses in the kitchen. "Keep your hand still," she said. She stroked him. He had gained weight. She had realized this while wrestling with him. The word hefty came to her mind. He lay there tense, she could feel the tension under his skin, a wary tension. His penis was small as it lay warm in her hand. He only relaxed when she left her hand lying quietly on his genitals. It was the first time since he had taken refuge with her that they didn't make love. Outside the birds were calling. She didn't sleep, he didn't sleep, but both pretended to be sleeping.

The next day, from old Wehrmacht supplies, she got hold of some ointment for his hand, which he kept in a sling. And she had another balm, a quite different one: She said an amnesty for deserters was being prepared, the date to be announced. Those who report voluntarily will not be punished. What bliss, he positively jumped for joy, grabbed her—"Watch out," she said, "remember your hand"—and whirled her around the kitchen: "Fabulous!"

And then she laid out on the kitchen table the things she had managed to obtain on the strength of nearly three years' experience of wangling, of persuasion, threats, promises, reciprocal back-scratching: four eggs, a kilo of potatoes, a liter of milk, a quarter pound of butter, and, most precious of all, half a nutmeg that she had acquired in exchange for five hundred paper napkins, highly prized for use as soft toilet paper. She put the potatoes on to boil and brought out the potato masher she hadn't used for over a year. She felt that, after the terrible fight that had so humiliated him, this was the only way to show him how very much she cared for him, how sorry she was about everything; and it seemed to her that with this his favorite food she could also dispel those first clouds, put an end to the apathetic downing of his food she had been noticing the last three or four days, that lethargic lying about with vacant eyes whenever his mind wasn't occupied with the latest tank advances.

"Obviously," said Mrs. Brücker, "the sky had fallen in on him. What else was there for him to do, cleaning up the kitchen, solving crossword puzzles, looking out the window?"

But now he cheered up. "A general amnesty. Man," he said, "man, oh man! At last!" And that day she wanted to serve him something very special, something substantial. Plenty of eggs. "He needed that, so much had been demanded of him!" she said. She laughed, dropped the blue strand, and looped the green one carefully over her finger.

"How do you manage to keep the strands apart?" I asked. "Sequence. You have to keep track of that. Sheer brain work. Keeps your mind young."

Bremer set the table, with napkins, and placed a candle in the middle, the one she kept for emergencies. After telling him to sit down, she served him two scoops of freshly mashed patatoes, well beaten and with no lumps, then carefully slid the four fried eggs onto his plate, drizzled some brown butter over them, and sat down across from him. She had served herself only a little of the mashed potato, saying: "I don't care for eggs," a downright lie. She watched him take the first mouthful of mashed potato with the precious brown butter; he tasted it, and for a moment a thoughtful, almost brooding look crossed his face. What's up, she thought, have I done something wrong? "Does it need salt?" she asked. "No." "Is something wrong?" she asked, realizing that he was comparing the flavor with what he remembered from his childhood.

As a matter of fact, though, he was trying to taste something, anything. It was at that point that he knew for sure that he had lost his sense of taste. It hadn't happened overnight, it had taken two or three days for him to become aware of it: the memory of flavors had lasted for a while before gradually starting to fade, though he could, as he told himself, be mistaken. But now he had the mashed potato and brown butter on his tongue, and he still had a pretty good idea of how that should taste—and he tasted nothing, nothing whatever. Of course he didn't say anything, he enthused over the mashed potato, enthused over the fried eggs whose yellow yolks the hot butter had turned into little brown islands, each in its ring of white. Yet—and this surprised Lena—he didn't mention the flavor of nutmeg. Surely that must strike him especially? For him it must be totally unfamiliar. Where could you still find nutmeg after five years of war? "Well," she asked, "what do you taste? A spice?" He replied evasively: "Simply fabulous."

There was a strange sensation on his tongue and gums, furry somehow, and numb, as if his tongue had gone to sleep. He explored with his tongue, ran the tip of it along his front teeth, felt what he had always felt, the smooth surfaces, the indented edges, only there was no taste, in fact nothing at all.

"What's the matter?" she asked.

"Nothing," but that nothing, uttered as it was with a probing, or rather wondering, baffled searching around his mouth, made her ask again: "Can't you taste it? I did give five hundred paper napkins for it, after all."

He shook his head. "I can't taste a thing."

"Nothing at all?"

"Nothing. For the last three or four days. Nothing at all." He stared at the plate, having made a clean sweep of its contents, and sat there looking the picture of misery.

They were lying side by side on the mattress island. She stroked his navel and picked out some bits of lint that had accumulated there from his underwear. "My hand hurts like hell," he said. "I can't support my weight on it." Oh, she thought, how many variations had they tried out where he didn't have to support his weight on his hands, but she said: "That's all right. It's nice just lying together like this."

"What can be done," she asked Holzinger, "when a person suddenly loses his sense of taste?"

Holzinger said: "It happens occasionally, a kind of plugging of the taste buds. They have to open up again. Who is it then?" he asked, giving her a searching look. Of course he first thought it must be one of the executives whose meals he prepared. That must be the highest culinary art, to be able to deprive repulsive characters and shit-heads of their sense of taste.

"A friend of mine."

"Has he lost his appetite?"

"No, not at all."

"Then it's the result of overindulgence."

"Hey, wait a minute!" Lena Brücker burst out, but then she collected herself and turned the angry outburst into a deeply worried question. "How does it happen?"

"An internal flaw," said Holzinger who, although from Vienna, had never read Freud. "A heaviness that comes from the heart."

"And what can be done about it?"

"Basil. Which we don't have. Even better, ginger, a spice for the treatment of depression. Which we most certainly don't have. Or coriander."

"Aha, curried sausage," I said, "is that it?"

Mrs. Brücker stopped knitting, looked at me, and

said rather sharply: "If you know so much, you tell the story."

"Captain Friedländer," I said.

"What about him?"

"You asked Captain Friedländer for some curry powder."

"Oh no, things are only that simple in novels. If it'd been the way you think, you'd never have been able to eat curried sausage. If Friedländer had had any curry powder, I might possibly have made curried rice, that's all. But never, never sausage. There were no sausages, you see. Besides, the British didn't have any curry powder either at that time. Supplies were only just starting to trickle in. And Friedländer said: 'Curry is horrible stuff. A kind of Indian Maggi.' Steamed meatballs, that's what he liked.

"You see?" she said, counting stitches. I waited. "You were on a completely wrong track. You must have a little more patience."

Bremer had all the time in the world. He had brought a chair to the window and put a thick cushion on it so he could sit a little higher but still be partially screened by the shade. He had placed a salt cellar on the windowsill to dip in his finger and lick it. He tasted nothing. He smelled nothing. The only stimulation was to his saliva glands. Down below a war amputee hobbled past on two crutches. How is it possible, he thought, to lose your sense of taste like a leg? He tried to find comfort in the thought that his sense of taste would return, just as, when he'd had worms as a boy and couldn't smell a thing, after the worm treatment his sense of smell had come back. He could hear the fast whizzing of a fighter plane in the sky. Maybe now they'll deploy the miracle weapon against the Russians. Maybe the robot plane. He had never believed in it until one day he saw the Me 136, the flying egg, the first rocket plane in the world, a small, rounded machine with little wing stumps that had soared up on a rocket stream through a bomber formation, then, in a swift dive, had shot down one, two, no less than three of those Flying Fortresses, after which it glided to earth, made a hard landing, and exploded. If the explosion at the end could be prevented, that's the miracle weapon, he had thought at the time. He picked up a little salt with his fingertip, just hoping that his sense of taste would come back again as suddenly as it had disappeared. He licked. Nothing. Maybe this is the price for running away, for deserting, for having been, no, being a coward. Strangely enough he was only now beginning to think seriously about his desertion, only now since he had lost his sense of taste. Maybe a person actually does permanently lose something when he surrenders or runs away, leaving others in the lurch; maybe something shatters inside him, something invisible yet solid, he thought. There'll be certain things I can no longer say, certain questions I'll avoid in future, assuming they don't eventually catch me—though they've abolished the SS there'll still be British and German MPs on their beat.

He smoked one of the precious English cigarettes and tasted nothing. His tongue had gone to sleep. Maybe, he thought, it comes from smoking, you smoke too much, but then immediately the thought crept in: It's not the smoking, it's that you've let a woman hide you here. You're a bastard, he thought.

"Could acorn coffee deaden the taste buds, tan them, so to speak, as my mother used to claim?" I asked Mrs. Brücker.

"Nonsense, utter nonsense. A rumor spread around at the time by the competition. My acorn coffee was especially good. The aroma was good because I always ground a few genuine coffee beans and added them to the ersatz coffee with a pinch of salt.

"No," she said, "the sky had simply fallen in on him. After all, he had to somehow get through more than nine hours alone in the apartment. The mornings were taken up with housework, sure, but the afternoons dragged. Even though there was more to be seen down on the street than before, because in addition to a few drab women lugging pails of water—which was no longer necessary anyway now that the waterworks were operating again—there was also quite a variety of types standing around, smartly dressed women from Eppendorf and Harvestehude who had come to barter the family silver here on Brüderstrasse. The harbor was nearby, and many people who lived in the area worked there. During loading and unloading, cases kept getting damaged, cigarettes suddenly lay scattered on the floor of the hold, coffee beans trickled from bags, and bananas dropped off their stalks. Racketeers stood down there in doorways, offering sides of bacon and sausages. Through the binoculars Bremer saw a silver tie clip in one man's hand. The hand slid it into a coat pocket and pulled out three smoked sausages, which were grasped by the hand of another man. And then that murmuring. During the first few days it had been barely audible, becoming clearer only when he cautiously opened the window. And when he did, it had to stay open until the evening. It was more of a whispering, a whispering that increased from day to day with the growing number of people, an unintelligible murmuring, an audible manifestation of what economists call supply and demand.

One afternoon Bremer was sitting in the kitchen, having that morning swept and mopped it, scraped out the corners with a knife, and finally applied a scrubbing brush to the floor. He was doing a cross-word puzzle. Germanic tribe, five letters: Suebi? Greek sorceress, five letters. First letter C. Didn't know that one. Suddenly the murmuring from below died away. Sound of a motor. He hurried to the window. A jeep was driving past at walking speed. In it sat two British MPs and two helmeted German police-men. The black market dealers had disappeared, or they were standing about in groups, pointedly chat-ting together as they looked up at the sky. All those people, though they had gathered quite randomly, had chosen to discuss the weather and were staring up in his direction. Bremer involuntarily took a step back.

That evening he told her about the jeep. British MPs accompanied by German policemen. "That, I believe, removed any doubt from his mind," said Mrs. Brücker. "The first few days the British had to rely on the German police for directions. They had to get to know the city, of course."

She had followed Holzinger's advice and fried up some potatoes with caraway seed and plenty of black pepper, which he had given her from his emergency stock. She set the plate on the kitchen table and watched Bremer stuff his mouth with the fried potatoes. Tears came to his eyes, and his nose began to run. He had to blow his nose several times. "D'you taste anything?" He merely shook his head and loosened his belt.

He had gained weight, quite considerably. This was due to lack of exercise, but also to Lena Brücker's skill at wangling supplies so that one man gained weight at a time when everybody else was losing it. To rustle up food supplies hadn't become any easier after the surrender. The British had taken charge of ration cards, just as they had of the food office, including Dr. Fröhlich. But friction arose between the producers—the farmers—and the authorities. And even among the authorities there was rivalry over distribution; fraud, profiteering, and theft increased. Not only because hoarders no longer had to fear the penitentiary or even the guillotine, but because the new administration was in the hands of the enemy. Only a few days earlier they had been at the enemy's throat. Perfidious Albion, those Tommies, ruled by plutocrats. Any means was justified to put one over on them, it wasn't one's own countrymen who were being gypped but the enemy.

She had made up her mind to tell Bremer the

truth that very evening. Holzinger had talked about his little girl who couldn't wait to get back in school— it was still closed. She had thought of the photograph of Bremer with his wife and child. While discussing the menu for the following day with Holzinger, she was wondering how to begin the conversation with Bremer. There were still several hundredweight of barley left, but Holzinger needed meat extract to give at least some flavor to the soup. "What's the matter with you?" Holzinger asked. "Hey there!" And he waved his hand in front of her eyes as if she were a child in a daydream. "You must try and dig up some meat extract. Ask Captain Friedländer. Give him the eye." I have to confess something. Confess? No, they only say that in movies. I want to tell you something. I have to clarify something. "What's wrong?" said Holzinger, "we still have onions. Of course meat would be better." The war is over, has been for days. For days? Yes, strictly speaking for three weeks, here in Hamburg. "I know that," said Holzinger. To say what has to be said. No, better: I must tell you I've been keeping something from you. But it was so hard to find the right words for that. How was she to put into simple words something so convoluted, so complex, with so many different, even contradictory reasons, simple words like: kept from you, in other words lied to you? "Almost," said Mrs. Brücker, "as if I had deceived him, although in that case I really hadn't, on the other hand I had. What a mess." "Hey," Holzinger asked, "are you even listening to me? I don't need a mess, I need some meat extract. Meat? Why not? Of course that would be fantastic. But I don't imagine you'll cut that out of your own ribs, will you? What's the matter with you?"

In the canteen, the two British officers were sitting at a white-clothed table, off to one side, together with a Swedish journalist who was planning an article on the supply situation in occupied Germany. Lena Brücker, in ladling out the Irish stew prepared by an English cook but tasting considerably worse than Holzinger's meat extract soup, splashed some of it on Captain Friedländer's uniform.

"Oh, I'm sorry! I'm all confused today."

"Never mind," he said.

She hurried to the kitchen, returned with a damp cloth, and began to clean up the uniform. "That's all right," he said, embarrassed in front of so many people. Later he slipped her a pack of cigarettes. "You're in trouble. Perhaps I can help you," he said, giving her a look that was forbidden—they were not allowed to fraternize, of course. "Perhaps," said Mrs. Brücker, "if it hadn't been for Bremer at that time I might be in England today, in one of those old folks' homes with ivy-covered walls."

She would, she told herself on her way home, unlock the door and say: You can leave if you like. The war's over. I've been extending it a bit for us—for you, but mainly for myself. For entirely personal, selfish reasons, I admit. I simply wanted to keep you here a little longer. That's the truth. She might say: You couldn't have seen your wife and child any earlier anyway. What interests me, by the way, what I've been wanting to ask you: Is it a girl or a boy? He would then also say something, she hoped. The worst thing would be if he were to leave the apartment without a word. Perhaps he'd say: Why did you lie to me like that? Or deceive me? That was exactly the right word for what had happened: She had moved around outside in a totally different world from the one he imagined. Perhaps he would say: It's wrong to extend the war, that's indecent, immoral. He had deserted, and she had helped him do so. She had prevented him from killing others, possibly from being killed himself. But she wouldn't say it like that. Never mind. As long as he said something to which she could make some reply, and then they could talk, about the time, the years, she had been alone, about his wife, about his daughter or his son. In any case she wanted to tell him what she had thought up on her long walk home: That even in the dark times there are bright moments, and that the darker the times are the brighter those moments seem.

And then she unlocked the apartment door.

And he didn't ask for newspapers, didn't ask for radio tubes, or about the position of the German troops. Instead he said: "Happy birthday" and led her to the kitchen table: there, carefully cut out of magazine paper and ingeniously folded, were three red paper flowers. Beautiful substitute roses.

"How did you know?"

"I saw your birth date on the coal-ration card."

The window was open, from below came the murmuring of the black-market dealers; it was so peaceful that she almost said: It's peace, it's all over and done with. You needn't be afraid anymore. But then she told herself that at this moment she didn't want to spoil either his mood or hers. Besides, once the truth was out she would have plenty of time to reflect, and she thought: Now I'll carefully ration the days for myself. I'll have the paper arrive two days earlier for him, that's in three days, and those three days will be for me. In that way we'll both be rewarded. And whatever she made up her mind to do—in forty years she had come to know herself well enough—she did.

6

BUT THEN, ON THE FOLLOWING DAY,
Lena Brücker saw the photographs. They had appeared in the newspaper. Photographs that took
away Lena Brücker's appetite—yet she had had nothing to eat that morning—photographs that caused her
to go home in a daze, that made her ask herself what
she had been seeing and thinking all those years, or
rather, what she had not been thinking and what she
had not wanted to see. They were the kind of photographs which at that time many, or most, or, to be
exact, all Germans were seeing. Photographs from the
concentration camps liberated by the Allies. Dachau,
Buchenwald, Bergen-Belsen. Freight cars filled with
skin-and-bones corpses. One picture showed the
captured guards—SS men and SS women—actually
loading the freight cars with these skeletons. Some of
the SS men had rolled up their sleeves and were
buckling down to the job. Camp survivors were sitting,
or rather lying, about apathetically, near death, in
striped uniforms.

When she reached home, Bremer asked her if she
wasn't feeling well. And she told him what she pretended to have heard in town. But, as she spoke it

seemed to her to be a lie, a dirty lie which tainted her. She told him she'd heard: There had been camps in which people had been killed, systematically killed, tens of thousands, hundreds of thousands, some said millions.

"Rumors," said Bremer.

She couldn't possibly say, I've seen it in black and white. I've seen pictures in the newspaper. Today for the first time the captain didn't speak to me, didn't say hello, didn't look at me, didn't offer me a cigarette. I had set the table for him, put some daffodils on the table specially for him. But he said nothing, nothing, he merely shook his head and disappeared into his office, closing the door behind him though he usually left it open.

"People, Jews," she told Bremer, forcing herself to remain calm, "are said to have been gassed and then cremated. Unimaginable things happened. They say there were death factories."

"Fairy tales," said Bremer, "all nonsense. Enemy propaganda. Who's interested in inventing such rumors? The Russians." And then he said something that deeply upset Lena Brücker. Mrs. Brücker had paused, her knitting in her lap, looked a little beyond me, shook her head: "Has Breslau been relieved yet?" he had asked.

At that, for the first and only time, she yelled at

him: "No! The city has gone to hell! Long ago. Flattened. Get it? Nothing left. District Leader Handke scrammed. In a Fieseler plane. A big bastard, just as this Dr. Fröhlich is a little bastard. They're all bastards. Everyone in uniform is a bastard. You and your stupid war games. The war's over. Get it? Over. Long ago. Finished. Washed up. We've lost it, totally. Thank God."

"There he stood, how shall I put it, looking at me, not horrified, not even puzzled, no, stupefied. And then I picked up my raincoat and left. I walked along the bombed-out streets, for a long time—I can think best when I'm walking. This had once been a beautiful city, and now it lay in ruins, rubble, and ashes, and I thought: That's how it should be, and then I thought: Maybe all that about the Jews really is enemy propaganda. Maybe it's not all true. Photographs can be faked too. No, not like that. There had been piles of corpses, ditches full of corpses, contorted, emaciated bodies, lying every which way, feet beside heads, bald heads, eye sockets, skulls. The mind refuses to believe it. But then I thought of the Jews I had known. They had disappeared. Some of them before the war, others, mostly older ones, during the war. I thought of Mrs. Levinson. A morning in 1942. Grossneumarkt. That's where the Joseph-Herz-Levy Foundation used to be. A home for needy Jews."

Lena Brücker had been on her way to the food office when she saw two army trucks parked outside the building. The old people stood in line with their valises and little cardboard suitcases and were being pushed on to the trucks. She caught sight of Mrs. Levinson, the widow of Mr. Levinson, owner of a drygoods store. An SS man took her suitcase from her as she climbed on the truck, pulled up from above by two gloved hands. Mrs. Levinson waved to Lena from the truck, the way a person waves when starting out on a journey, but furtively. Mrs. Levinson was then seventy-six and was wearing the little black velvet hat she was always seen in. Lena Brücker had waved back, furtively, so furtively that later, on her way to work, she felt ashamed. And of course she had wondered where all those people would be taken to. And everyone guessed, somewhere in the east, to concentration camps. There they disappeared. The east was vast. *Lebensraum*, that was the east.

A railway employee, a stoker called Lengsfeld, who had at one time worked on the tugboats on the Elbe, lived on Brüderstrasse and when the war broke out he had been recruited for service on the railroad. One day Lena Brücker ran into him on the street, and he told her that every day freight trains filled with people were heading east. Not a sound came from the trains. Sometimes, when the trains stopped at a freight yard, you could see hands sticking through the air vents of the cattle cars. The hands were begging for bread and water. And then. What and then? And then, shoes and dentures kept turning up beside that railway line. Dentures? Yes. But why? Haven't the faintest, said the stoker. On the way they throw their dentures out of the cars. But why? Haven't the faintest, said the stoker.

It had stopped raining, and she had gone home. She wanted to talk to Bremer, wanted to try and explain everything to him.

She opened the apartment door. He wasn't standing in the corridor, or sulking at the kitchen table, or fuming in the living room or the bedroom. She ran to the storeroom. It was empty. In the cupboard her husband's gray suit was missing. What hung there was Bremer's uniform, carefully brushed, with the strange equestrian badge. She looked for a note, a letter, a message. Nothing.

Strangely enough, what tormented her was not that he had left but that she hadn't had a chance to talk to him about why she had kept quiet about the surrender. Above all she would have liked to tell him that her silence hadn't done him any harm. He couldn't have left much sooner. Even now he might still be picked up and sent to prison camp, since if stopped by the military police he would be asked to produce his discharge papers, when he had actually discharged himself.

On the other hand, he won't be conspicuous in his gray suit. The higher-up Nazis dressed as farm workers or put on uniforms of the lower ranks. And now, she thought, he won't have to send back the suit anymore. That, at least, she told herself, was some relief for the moment. He hadn't borrowed the suit, he'd exchanged it. And as for whatever story he told his wife, she didn't care. For the story, her story, was something he couldn't tell anybody; it wasn't one of those war stories that kept going the rounds. It wasn't a story to be bandied about with barroom buddies.

It's a story that only I can tell. For there are no heroes in it.

She walked through the kitchen and saw the butts he had tipped into the garbage pail. He had washed and put away the dishes. The sink had been cleaned. And in the corridor, neatly folded, lay the tarpaulin under which she had walked home with him in the rain.

She sat down at the kitchen table and wept.

"I think," she said, "now the sun should begin to rise." She held the unfinished part of the sweater out to me.

"Yes."

"Shall I add a white cloud, a little cushiony cloud?"

"That would be nice."

"I'll think about it. Put some water on."

I turned on the heating coil in the kitchenette. She wanted to make the coffee herself, she insisted on that. When the coffee had passed through the filter she added more water. Standing there absorbed, never saying a word, she listened to the dripping as it gradually slowed down. Her eyes were fixed on the plastic imitation-tile wallpaper.

I slid the wedge of torte onto a plate. She walked to the table. "Real coffee," she said. "So don't worry about your tongue getting tanned and all that."

"So what happened to Bremer?" I urged.

"No idea," she said.

"I thought curried sausage had something to do with Bremer."

"It did. But not directly. It was a coincidence. I stumbled. That's all. Although—the older you get the less you believe in coincidences." After carefully carrying the coffeepot to the table, she felt first for my cup, then hers, and poured. And again I was amazed that she could fill the cups so evenly.

"Well, first of all the men returned from the prison camps. In January '46 Last-Ditch Fröhlich was released from internment camp and then denazified as a mere fellow traveler. In this case, the biter saw to it that he wasn't bitten. Although he was no longer general manager, but personnel manager instead. Get it?

"And then one day, in March '46, the doorbell rings, and there he stands."

"Bremer?"

"No, my husband."

I didn't need to hide anything from her, of course, my sinking back in the chair, shaking my head, I also could have rolled my eyes theatrically toward the ceiling or clasped my brow. And yet she seemed to have noticed something: perhaps I had given an involuntary little gasp. Her hearing was certainly extremely acute.

"My husband," she said, "is also part of the story."

"Really?"

"Yes."

"But the day after tomorrow I have to go back to Munich. The children are complaining, so is my wife.

And they're right. I meant to spend only a week in Hamburg, and this is already the second week."

"Can't you postpone your return for a day or two?"

"Impossible."

"What a pity," she said, "it really is a pity, we'll have to cut it short, the story about Gary. It's specially interesting. Gary, you see, thought up the Paradox Ball—that dance café where the women ask the men to dance, and the men aren't allowed to refuse." The idea was later stolen from him by Mrs. Keese.

"I'll be coming back to Hamburg quite often—you must tell me the story then."

But she maintained an obstinate silence and continued slicing morsels from her cherry torte with her cake fork. Her movements were slow, due to her age, but they were precise, and because they were so slow one didn't notice how systematically the first piece of torte had disappeared. Then, for a change of pace, she put a little piece of ripe Gouda in her mouth, sucking on it as if it were candy. I slid a second piece of torte onto her plate. "Fabulous," she said, and went on eating.

I was silent and waited patiently.

Outside, gusts of wind forced the rain against the window.

"So your husband Gary came back." In a tone simulating keen curiosity, I tried to start her talking again. "From where?"

"From Russian POW camp. He was in splendid shape, unlike other POWs returning from Russia. He'd been given special rations because he could play Russian folk songs on his comb. The prison guards must've cried their eyes out.

"So in comes Gary. Jürgen, my son, is sitting in the kitchen. The Americans had released him very quickly. Still a kid, at sixteen. Apprentices weren't being taken on yet. Jürgen worked at a conveyor belt, sorting whole and half bricks from the rubble. Always been a hard-working boy. 'Hello,' said Gary. Jürgen sits transfixed at the table. A man comes in and says: 'I'm your father.' Jürgen hadn't seen him since he was ten. Gary tries to hug me. 'Just a moment,' I said and sent the boy out of the room, then: 'What do you want here?'

"'Are you kidding? To look after the kids, of course.'

"'That's a laugh,' was all I said.

"Then he went to the cupboard and brought out his blue suit. 'Where's the gray one?'

"'I exchanged it.'"

She had said this quite brazenly and shown him

the naval uniform. He stared at the uniform jacket. Had a good look at it. And his expression revealed his inner struggle, how he was wondering what he should do, for whatever he said would decide the whole future. Was he to be furious, was he to say what probably many men would have said and did say: While I had to risk my neck you're in bed having fun with another man? But he will also have thought that that was exactly what he mustn't say. She could simply have responded: Where were you all that time? And as for risking your neck, don't make me laugh.

"At that moment I wasn't even flustered," said Mrs. Brücker, carefully picking up her knitting from the table.

"He fingered the Narvik shield, then the equestrian badge. He wanted to say something, make some silly joke, and I thought, If he does that I'll kick him out on the spot."

He looked at her and noticed her lower lip tightening and that she was staring at him, fixing him with an expression: Come on, say it, then all hell will break loose.

"'Fine,' he said, 'now we're even.'"

Even—what a laugh, she thought, you'd have to add at least twelve years and a hundred men. She swallowed her words and said nothing.

One month later the canteen manager was released from prison. Dr. Fröhlich sent for Lena Brücker. Sitting at his desk he merely said: "You're redundant now, right?" "Can I at least work as a waitress?" With a sly grin Fröhlich said: "There are enough hands around to clean up the mess."

Lena Brücker went home, where from now on she cooked, cleaned, and was reminded of Bremer, who had cleaned the place and washed the dishes, going repeatedly—as she did now—to the window to look down. In contrast to him she was free to go downstairs anytime, yet she felt imprisoned. *Once I managed a canteen, was with other people, it was a good time: phoning and getting hold of supplies. The people from the fish market would say: Hello Mrs. Brücker, we've four cases of cod today, and the man from the unrationed section: Nothing today, I had to supply the police headquarters canteen, but tomorrow's your turn again, how've you been keeping? The man from the agricultural co-op would phone: I've a shipment of damaged lettuce today, the very thing for your pen-pushers! And give a nasty laugh.* Now she sat at home, looking after Heinz the baby who Edith, her daughter, had brought from Hanover, without a father. More and more often, in the afternoon, when the cleaning and shopping had all been done and everything put away, she was overcome by a feeling of being stifled. Then she would sometimes look down at the kitchen floor, at the spot where the mattress raft had lain, where they had drifted, naked, telling each other about themselves, or rather, she had told him about herself.

"Those days," said Mrs. Brücker, looking slightly beyond me with her milky eyes, "were happiness."

From the corridor came a faint squeaking. "Mrs. Lüdemann's wheelchair." Voices. An elevator starting up. A distant cough.

"For a while I substituted one for the other, in my mind anyway. I only had to close my eyes. That works, but just for a while. Slowly loses effect. And then he gradually becomes the one who's really lying on top of you. You smell it, feel it, can't fight it even with your eyes tight shut."

During the week Gary was on the road with his truck, driving for the British military authorities, transporting lathes and other machine tools which the Tommies dismantled and sent to England. Sometimes he carried food supplies. Came home Friday evening with a bag full of dirty laundry. But always brought something to eat too.

Went to bed and slept like a log, without snoring, hardly moving. On Saturdays Gary sat on the sofa, unshaven, his feet up, drinking beer and leafing through magazines. Toward evening he lathered his face, gave himself a close shave, powdered his face, and tinted his graying eyebrows: he had his barber dye his eyelashes. He really did look like Gary Cooper, with his flashing blue eyes, even to the pouches under them, only that her Gary looked somewhat the worse for drink, even in those days. Then he'd put on his hand-tailored shirt, his suit, ask with mock-politeness if she'd like to come along, no thanks, then take his comb from his pants pocket and play "Goodbye, sweetheart," and off he'd go to one of the bars where there was music and drinking, where Americans and Tommies would hang around with some hick females who were seeking their fortune with their bosoms and backsides. Wanted to get away from hunger, rubble, cold. California—that's where they all wanted to go, next came the east coast, last of all Liverpool.

He'd come home late at night reeking of schnapps and beer and smoke, and sometimes his hand would creep like a spider under the quilt and up her legs, which always jolted her awake. "Probably thought he must be nice to me. A quickie. Each time it was like a cold rock in my stomach."

After three months she began to make excuses, told him she had a yeast infection. She'd had one ten years before, and suddenly they had both started itching whenever they slept together. After that the hand stopped creeping. Now she could sleep undisturbed as long as he didn't snore too loudly, and that got going only on Saturday nights. Funny, wasn't it? Or when he came home at night and was so drunk he peed against the bedside table.

Then—one Friday evening early in November—he arrived, put down the bag of underwear as usual, had four beers, and fell into bed.

On Saturday he sat in the living room, slippers on his feet, looking through a dog-eared magazine. Lena Brücker was busy soaking the washing in the galvanized washtub—everything still had to be washed by hand, of course. She placed the washboard in the tub and scrubbed a pair of his underpants, especially the place where his shit had dried up in a brown streak. Then pulled the next underpants out of the soapy water. They were a woman's. White ones that fit a bit, no, much more snugly than hers. Under a tight skirt the elastics—tight, very tight—would imprint the backside with that heart-shaped outline she knew Gary was so fond of. From the big washtub she fished out a pair of her own underpants. Held it beside the other pair. How wide hers were, they looked like wings. If she were to jump out the window in them, they would flap around her legs. She stood there staring at her hands in the washtub, their backs reddened by the hot water, the fingers white and wrinkled.

Just then her husband called out: "Go get me a bottle of beer, cold." He insisted that she go to the bar at the corner and pick up some cold beer—in those days they didn't have a refrigerator. She lifted her hands out of the water, went to the kitchen table, slowly opened the drawer containing all the bread knives and meat knives, then abruptly closed it again. She called out: "Have a look outside, Gary, I think there was a knock." He hadn't heard anything but went to the door. It was dark in the stairwell. He switched on the light, and just as he leaned over the banister to look down she slammed the apartment door behind him. Standing outside, he rang the bell, knocked, hammered, and finally kicked at the door. He was in a towering rage. She braced herself against the inside of the door. Suddenly the palm of his hand appeared through the letter slot, the fingers moving like the arms of a crab as he tried to get hold of the handle. At that she screamed. She heard voices from the stairwell, heard Claussen shouting from below: "Quiet up there!" And because her husband kept on shouting Claussen could be heard coming up the stairs, his heavy tread, a man built like a tank, a man who could bend five-mark pieces.

"Quiet, or I'll fix you, dammitall!"

Outside the door it was now quiet. She could hear the stairs creaking. Claussen the dredge skipper walked down the stairs, followed by her husband, who was in his shirt and pants, wearing his slippers. She stood behind the curtain at the kitchen window, staring down onto Brüderstrasse, the short stretch that could be seen from above, the section of pavement, the sidewalks. She watched him as he passed by below, without looking up, shuffling off in his slippers. He never came back.

From then on she was left in peace, though she had two children to look after. Her daughter Edith still hadn't found a job. And then there was Heinz, the baby. The baby's father, Edith's boyfriend, a lieutenant in the engineer corps, was still missing, not in Russia but in Brandenburg. "Crazy, wasn't it?"

I had to get her away from Edith and the missing lieutenant and bring her back to the curried sausage. "There's a bit of a west wind blowing," I told her, "with rain on and off. How about a drive to Grossneumarkt? We could have some curried sausage, couldn't we?"

"It'll be such a hassle again."

"No, it won't" I said, "we can park there, that's no problem."

"And then that wishy-washy curried sausage. No thanks."

But then she changed her mind, I believe because of the simple desire to walk once more across the square where for thirty years she had had her booth, going there each morning and staying until the evening. Closed only on Sundays. For thirty years no vacation, never missed a day. Even when it was snowing she had fried sausages, sold beer, put pickles on paper plates. She wanted to hear the sounds, to smell the Elbe—yes, you can smell the Elbe there when there's a west wind: brackish water, oil, drains, red lead, accompanied by the clanging and clanking from the shipyards, riveting hammers, the ships' sirens.

She had put on her green mackintosh again and pulled the plastic rain bonnet over her brimless brown hat.

I drove her past the building she had lived in for more than forty years, the front door that had opened and shut behind the shuffling husband, the top-floor window where the imprisoned Bremer had stood looking down.

I described the Alter Steinweg to her, all clean and freshly painted, the window frames and sills white, the façades in a pale shade of gray.

"Across the street there's now a Spanish restaurant." "Spanish?" "Yes," I said. "At the corner there's an office-furniture design business." We turned onto Wexstrasse. "Mr. Zwerg's tobacco store is still there. Mr. Zwerg is standing behind the display case, polishing his glass eye. D'you want me to stop?"

"No," she said, "don't bother."

Brüderstrasse, Wexstrasse, that was where the black market had been. From there those people had gone across to Grossneumarkt, to her stand, racketeers and small-time dealers alike, to fortify themselves, a lemonade, an acorn coffee, a fried sausage, or perhaps some curried sausage.

"Curried sausage?" I asked cautiously, "even in those days?"

"Well sure, it was very popular. Business was good, better than it ever was later," she said. "That's to say, '68 was good too. When the students used to come. But after that it went downhill, McDonald's arrived with their soft buns, and then the kebab places. But '47, those were the days. No one paid with money, it was all barter. Depending on the rate of the day, a curried sausage and a cup of genuine coffee were worth three or four American cigarettes. Of course you could eat on credit, too. Regular customers. Accounts were settled at the weekend, with sugar, chocolate, lard. Complicated. But that was what I enjoyed, a person had to have a good nose for it." She raised her head, looked toward me with her milky blue eyes, and touched her nose. "The point was, nothing was settled with money, you had to know what was in demand, what the shortages were." At her stand, more important transactions also took place while people were having their coffee and curried sausage. Her stand was a meeting-point, a kind of open-air stock exchange. For example, eighteen slabs of Virginia tobacco for twenty-two cases of smoked herring, a demijohn of pure alcohol, four badly worn automobile tires, or twenty kilos of Danish butter. The skill lay in correctly assessing the value, in other words the supply and demand, of such varied items as Danish butter, smoked herrings, and tobacco slabs. And even as you were assessing, all the rates were changing, of course. The currency was the cigarette—not just any cigarette but a Chesterfield or a Players.

Which definitely has its intrinsic logic, I would think, for that cigarette-currency was not only in demand, generally uniform and not perishable, but also esthetically pleasing: cylindrical, white, light-weight. Above all, it had a consumption value, not like the Reichsmark which, since it was losing its value, was only good for lighting a cigarette. Nor was it by chance that no other object of consumption value was considered—nourishing and perishable and hard to transport, like butter and lard—apart from the cigarette, light little cylinders that fit into every jacket pocket. The value of the cigarette, something neither nourishing nor useful, lies solely in its consumption, to be dissipated in aroma and smoke, with a flavor that calms the nerves. All that remained of this exchange value, when actually realized in terms of the chaotic black market, was a few ashes. I went more than once to that black market with my father, an addicted smoker. And probably way back then I stood at Mrs. Brücker stand. But my father would never have dreamed of eating curried sausage, let alone buying me one.

"How did you come by the stand?" I asked Mrs. Brücker. "It was a tip from Mrs. Claussen. The owner was an old man who made potato pancakes mixed with sawdust. Real belly-fillers. He had a stroke and couldn't lug the potatoes anymore. Had to rent out the stand: two loaves of bread and a pound of butter a week."

She had gone there and carefully looked it over. A wooden shack. An old ship's tarp stretched over it which leaked when it rained. She thought of the tarpaulin left behind by Bremer, still lying in the storeroom exactly as he had folded it. She could stretch that over the stand. Then she'd be out of the rain.

The problem was to get hold of something edible. The old man had a brother who was a farmer. She had to come up with something. Maybe veal sausage made from white cabbage.

"Can that be done?"

"Sure, it's all a matter of flavoring."

I parked the car on Grossneumarkt and helped her get out, reassuring her that we had plenty of time.

Through the rain I led her slowly over the cobblestones. The flower stall was still there. There weren't many people on the square. Three tramps were sitting on a bench under a plastic sheet and drinking red wine out of a straw-covered bottle.

"Well, is the food stand still there?"

"Yes, I mean no, it's not a stand. It's a big trailer, a kind of camper, painted white, with four wheels, technically state-of-the-art, equipped with stainless-steel sink, fridge, grill, sausage steamer, frypan." This van bore no resemblance to Mrs. Brücker's old wooden shack and her heavy iron pans.

"Two curried sausage."

The man took a sausage and stuffed it into a little machine: the slices fell out of the bottom. Then he stuffed in the next one.

"What's that noise?"

"A sausage-slicer," the man explained, "bought it a month ago. But they've had these in Berlin for a long time. Here in Hamburg we're always behind the times."

For a moment I wondered whether I shouldn't

say: Standing in front of you is the inventor of curried sausage, but then I remembered that I still had no answer to the question of how and when she had invented it. Mrs. Brücker was silent too. She looked quite rakish in her brimless brown hat under the plastic rain bonnet. She stared at the white wall of the van.

"How's business?" she asked.

"Not too good, when it's raining it's lousy."

"How long have you had this spot?"

"Three years, used to be in Münster. I want to go back. This isn't a good area. Too many smart asses. None of them would ever eat curried sausage." He pushed the paper plates across to us. "That'll be six eighty."

The sausage was cold from the ketchup slapped onto it, and the curry powder, made in Oldenburg, was only sprinkled on top. A pork sausage with little transparent bluish specks, remains of gristle and bristles. I gave Mrs. Brücker a two-pronged plastic fork and guided her hand to the paper plate. She speared a piece of sausage. She chewed slowly, pensively. Her expression gave no sign as to how she liked it. An old man came up and ordered a beer and a breaded schnitzel. At that moment Mrs. Brücker knocked the paper plate with the curried sausage off the table. I picked up the plate with the mess of curry, ketchup, and the cigarette butts sticking to it and tossed it all into the garbage can.

"Just leave it there," said the van owner, "the dog'll eat it."

7

ON THURSDAY, MY LAST DAY IN Hamburg, I brought Mrs. Brücker a Madeira cake. She insisted that we have some right away. Hugo arrived, bringing the three pink pills, and was given a slice. He inspected the front half of the sweater as it lay on the table. The hill was rounded, the tip of the fir tree had reached the sky, and a small yellow arc heralded the growing ball of the sun. "Fantastic," he said. He couldn't finish his coffee because his pager summoned him to the lower floor: Old Mr. Teltow was wandering about the corridors again.

"How many stitches till I get to the sun?" I counted thirty. She looped the blue sky strand over her finger, letting the sun strand hang down, and began to knit. Without my having to prompt her with questions, she picked up her story exactly where she had left off the day before. It had been clear to her that she couldn't make a go of it with white-cabbage sausages. Holzinger told her about a woman, an alcoholic, who owned a sausage factory in Elmshorn.

That very evening Lena Brücker began to turn Bremer's uniform into a tailored suit. As she cut, she was literally making an incision in her own life. She took the uniform jacket apart. As she did so, she sang, which otherwise she never did because she sang so terribly off-key, never hitting the right note. Edith came and asked: "Who's singing? Suddenly you can really sing." "Of course." And she sang, in a steady voice and with all the right notes, The Lorelei. Then she bent once more over the pattern. Thank God navy pants were wide-bottomed, so there was enough material for a gored skirt. She could adapt the jacket to her figure by tucks at the waist, but across the chest she had to leave the two top buttons undone. In the mirror she saw that this didn't detract from her appearance as a serious businesswoman: a navy-blue suit with brass buttons which, since they had an anchor and no swastika, she could use.

At the end of October, on a Thursday, Lena Brücker squeezed herself onto an overcrowded express train to Elmshorn, where she asked her way to the Demuth sausage factory. Next to the factory stood the owner's villa. Lena Brücker asked to be announced and was received by a gray-haired lady whose face revealed no alcoholic excesses. Lena Brücker introduced herself as a food-stand owner, who needed fifty genuine veal sausages per business day, genuine ones, not stretched with pork and not enriched with sawdust or used window-putty. Mrs. Demuth asked whether she had a purchasing permit.

No. But she could offer a bottle of whiskey weekly for the three hundred sausages. Mrs. Demuth gave the matter some thought. Was that genuine English whiskey or just a German imitation? Lena Brücker said bravely, genuine Scotch whiskey. Mrs. Demuth swallowed and finally said: All right. But three hundred was too many. Two hundred and fifty. That was the utmost she could offer.

Lena Brücker mulled it over. Veal sausages were a luxury item of the first order, something altogether exceptional. People would scramble for them. If she were to sell a sausage for two cigarettes plus one Reichsmark, that would amount to five hundred genuine American cigarettes, and for three hundred it was possible to get a good adulterated whiskey in the original Scotch bottles. That meant a weekly profit of three hundred American cigarettes plus three hundred Reichsmark.

She traveled back on an overcrowded train, standing outside on the running board while clinging to the handholds. It was a mild fall day, but even so the air that was blowing through her hair made her hands first cold, then icy, and finally numb. Thank God the navy material was good prewar quality, pure wool. But now she was sorry she hadn't worn a coat. Hers had seemed so shabby, in fact bad for business. And it annoyed her that she had turned the pants into a skirt, for the wind blew under it, and whenever she felt cold down there she needed to pee. She should have done that before the train left but had decided to make sure of a place on the running board. She rode along, unable to think of barter, sausages, or whiskey. Instead she was concentrating wholly on holding back her pee, which for women with their short ureters is much more difficult than for men. The telegraph wires swung past. She tired to take her mind off her problem by counting the poles, 327, 328, 329. Beside her stood a man in a Luftwaffe leather coat, a rucksack on his back. He told her he was returning from a barter trip and had exchanged family silver for butter and bacon from a farmer. It must be seen to be believed, how expert those farmers had become. They look at the cutlery and say, Danish silver, art nouveau. "It's a fact. Have you heard this one? A barterer comes to a farmer's wife and shows her a Picasso. 'No thanks,' she says, 'we only collect Braque.'"

At that point Lena Brücker laughed out loud, laughing not at the joke, because Braque meant nothing to her, but laughing in relief, louder and louder because at last, at last, she peed away and felt the warm stream running down her legs.

Looking down she saw that the wind had also sprinkled the man's pant leg. The man asked suspiciously why she was laughing so uncontrollably.

"I'm wetting myself!" she finally managed to say.

"Did you bring off such a good deal?"

"Yes. I'm going into business for myself."

She turned her face into the wind. The sun shone as if behind milk glass. In a meadow a horse got to its feet and galloped away from the train. At that moment Lena Brücker remembered something else she could barter: Bremer's silver equestrian badge.

That very evening Lena Brücker went to see her friend Helga, whom she had known at the food office. Helga had a valuable asset: she spoke perfect English. Scarcely was the ban on fraternization lifted than she met an English major. This major collected German medals and decorations. A collector of a caliber such as only the English could produce. With a sense for the unusual. Not like the trusting Texan GI's on whom you could palm off three of Göring's uniform caps at the same time, all different sizes. The major had already built up an impressive collection: Iron Crosses First and Second Class, black, silver, and gold, close-combat bars of every category, the German Cross in Gold (pierced by a bullet), the Narvik shield, medals for U-boat and mini-U-boat crews, frogmen, but also such unusual decorations as the Knight's Cross with Swords and Oakleaves—he still lacked the one with diamonds—and now he heard of the silver equestrian badge.

He made a special trip to Brüderstrasse, climbed the three flights of stairs, and held the badge in his hand, that very badge that Boatswain Bremer had left behind with his naval uniform, that most unwarlike badge on which a man is raising his horse in a levade. Genuine whiskey, that made him laugh. He was looking for that himself. But he could offer lumber. The British military authorities had assigned him to supervise the Lauenburg forests, which were being cut down, sawed into boards, and shipped to England as reparation payment. Lena Brücker told her friend to ask the major what he could offer for the silver equestrian badge. A souvenir. Helga spoke to him, and the major tucked his swagger stick under his left arm, drew the beautifully soft, brown leather glove off his right hand, and picked up the silver equestrain badge, which Lena Brücker had polished until it sparkled. Then he said: "Well," adding something in English that her friend translated as twenty-four cubic meters of lumber, which was a very large amount, as her friend continued to translate. Again he said something, and her friend translated: Sawed into boards or squared lumber. At that Lena Brücker said: "Okay."

At home she read in her encyclopedia (People's Edition): One cubic meter equals a cube one meter long in each direction. So, if the lumber were delivered to her, it would take up a floor space of six times four or three times four meters, in which case it would be two meters high. She got a shock. So much all at once. For a little badge like that. But then the forest and lumber didn't belong to the English major. Where was she to put all that lumber? She'd simply have to exchange it for something even before it was delivered. She didn't want to go into the lumber business: she wanted to get the sausages. Besides, she had to rustle up some oil for the potato pancakes she intended to include in her offerings, pure vegetable oil, not what was recently fobbed off on Mrs. Claussen: used motor oil.

Vegetable oil—a racketeer who had been recommended to Lena Brücker, said he knew someone who could help her, though he was sure that person didn't need any lumber. He had in mind the British commissary in charge of the entire supply depot in Soltau, a bald-headed dwarf and an albino, but he had a wife who. . . . —and the racketeer kissed his fingertips with their manicured nails. Red-gold hair, long-legged. Rugs, silver, garnets, that's what he was after, that albino laid everything at his wife's feet—it was the only way he could get to her.

The ball of blue wool fell from Mrs. Brücker's lap and rolled across the room. I picked it up for her.

"Rewind it for me, but properly, please, so it won't get tangled."

That, if nothing else, was a lead, for Lena Brücker had heard of a man who had arrived from the Soviet occupation zone with three hundred squirrel skins, which in turn some Russian staff officer had brought from Siberia. This man wanted to exchange the skins for chloroform but had no interest in either squared lumber or boards. She was given a tip: The head of a gynecological clinic was looking for lumber to repair the attic and floors of his burned-out villa.

Now she still had to set a bait for the commissary, or rather his wife, in order to get her hands on the whiskey, as well as the tomato ketchup and the oil for the potato pancakes. She had decided to add less sawdust but on the other hand to raise the price.

If she succeeded she would have a workable equation. She asked the racketeer to arrange a meeting with the commissary and his wife; then she set up a time with Helga, who was to act as interpreter, and took the train to Othmarschen, where the owner of the squirrel skins lived, a former tank-corps colonel and holder of the Knight's Cross with Oakleaves. Lena Brücker sat with Helga in the dim, oak-furnished living room. The wife of the one-legged colonel set two glasses of sparkling elderberry wine in front of them. The doorbell rang, and in came the commissary. He was a little man but by no means a dwarf, nor was he bald and certainly not an albino. The wife, on the other hand, had been correctly described by the racketeer: red-gold hair, eyebrows beautifully curved, and a complexion with the transparent pallor and clarity of porcelain. And her limbs—she was a head taller than the commissary—were slender: her fingers and arms, and—without being skinny—her legs.

She was wearing a gray Persian-lamb coat and a matching tricorne hat with a large mother-of-pearl shell on the brim. The colonel greeted the commissary's wife with a gallant kiss of the hand, something he had not done with Lena Brücker or her friend Helga. Then he brought in the squirrel skins, which had already been tanned. The commissary's wife let the little skins slide through her hands. Wonderfully soft gray skins with snow-white bellies and little black-tipped tails, and Lena Brücker in her businesslike suit could tell at once: That woman would never give up those skins, desire was creeping softly into her fingers, into her palm, and from there up her back into her head. And what she felt in the palm of her hand issued from the painted mouth as a velvety, voluptuous sound: "Marvelous." A word that Lena Brücker couldn't understand, yet did understand, for its effect on the man, whom the woman called

"Kiess" (for Keith) was a nod of the head. Through Helga, the commissary asked what Lena Brücker wanted for a finished coat.

She had written it all down and handed him her slip of paper: 20 liters of pure vegetable oil, 30 bottles of ketchup, 20 bottles of whiskey, and 10 cartons of cigarettes.

"*Toooo* much," he said. And Lena Brücker, without knowing a single word of English, realized what that meant. With a silver mechanical pencil he began to jot down some figures on the paper, figures that she in turn adjusted, then back to the commissary again: 20 liters of pure vegetable oil, 30 bottles of ketchup, 10 bottles of whiskey, 5 cartons of cigarettes.

For the second time Lena Brücker said: "Okay."

With that the circular barter could begin. She bartered the silver equestrian badge for the lumber, the lumber for the chloroform, the chloroform for the squirrel skins.

Now she still had to find someone who could make the skins into a coat. My aunt, who lived downstairs in her building, recommended my father who, having found a fur-sewing machine in the ruins of a building, was in the process of becoming a furrier.

So that's how my father came into the story. After his release from a British POW camp he bartered his

Russia-leather riding boots for food and, in order to survive, began to repair fur coats. But could he, without ever having made a coat, produce a squirrel coat?

"Yes," she said, "I was scared. I had invested my entire capital, you see."

My father also had frightening dreams at that time, nightmares of a fur coat that turned out much too short, all askew, and sewn together at the bottom like a sack.

At last I could ask my question: "What was he like, what was your impression of him in those days— I mean, my father?"

"Well, let's just say, how shall I put it, like a person who's seen better days. A bit of a martinet.

"And," she paused to reflect, "like someone who has already made many squirrel coats."

This is one of my early memories of my father. He is sitting in an army overcoat dyed green, wearing an army cap dyed blue, cutting out the front paws in ovals, then closing up the holes on the fur-sewing machine. He is cursing, but under his breath. He brushes the skin sides with water, pulls and tugs each piece of fur into the proper shape, pins down each one separately, cuts away the surplus, and sews the pieces together. This creates a pattern of white blending into medium gray and then, in the center of each skin, into a soft dark gray. But each movement of the fur skins is a shifting gray, now darker, now lighter. He had bought a book, *The German Furrier*, a manual to which he keeps referring. Following the illustrated example, he designs a pattern, measures, and calculates. The measurements had been sent to him: the commissary did not want a stranger, especially not "a German," to touch his wife, in other words, take her measurements. My father reads: *The sewn strips of skin are now adjusted along the edges; then the strips are sorted, stitched together, and placed on the paper pattern. Dampen the skin sides well with water, and pin the skins onto a large wooden board. The rows of skins must be straightened with pins. Allow them to dry. Remove the pins, adjust the edges again, then baste them together.*

More than once he had to laboriously unpick seams because tufts of the ultra-fine hairs had been caught in the stitching. I can still hear him cursing under his breath. And my body has another memory: I am allowed to sleep with my mother in the only bed in the room, while my father spends the night on the pinning-board, covered by his overcoat. In the light from the kerosene lamp the frozen water glistens on the cellar wall, a magical, wonderful landscape—seen from the warm bed.

Then, after a week, the day for the fitting arrived. The sleeves had been basted in, the collar sewn on, only the lining was still lacking. The day felt fit for a ship-launching, and it was a Friday.

Mrs. Brücker was also at the fitting. That morning the first sausages had been delivered to her in good faith. And as she unpacked them she discovered: "They've no skins!" "Yeah," said the driver, "no casings, we got none." He had to drive on, to the British military hospital, which was also being supplied by the sausage factory. "The British are quite happy with the sausages the way they are. They eat them as kind of skinless hotdog." Skinless veal sausages—that meant the sausages would dry out in the pan. Mrs. Brücker had brought us three. Without fat they actually tasted somewhat bland. But still good.

Before the commissary's wife arrived, Mrs. Brücker, who was the same height as the Englishwoman although heavier, wanted to try on the coat. Light as a feather it was, she hardly knew she had it on, yet it warmed her like a down quilt. Lena Brücker stood before the full-length mirror, which was cracked from top to bottom, and saw herself as she had never seen herself before and would never see herself again, like a film star; even the fine gray streaks in her hair, which had appeared after Bremer's departure, looked as if skillfully dyed to harmonize with the exquisite nuances shifting between the pale gray and the soft white strips of the fur coat. For an instant as she looked at herself in the mirror, she hesitated: Should she simply keep the coat? After all, strictly speaking she would have acquired it for that silver equestrian badge of Bremer's, and she realized at that moment that she would never be able to afford anything as extraordinary as this squirrel coat. But then she thought of the food stand, which was to provide her with a living, and of her son, who had to finish his apprenticeship as a chimney sweep, and of the baby Heinz, her grandson, who would soon be needing his first shoes. So she took the coat off.

"Lovely," she said, "it's turned out just lovely."

They were sitting in the cellar, smoking, Mrs. Brücker and my father. After Bremer's stay with her she had become an occasional smoker, three cigarettes a month, five at most. My father smoked eighty a day. He had made the coat for four cartons of cigarettes and two kilos of butter, and she gave him a pack of Players as a bonus. She looked at the coat on its hanger. The first coat my father ever made in his life. It looked simply beautiful: after all, it was a squirrel coat such as most furriers never get their hands on in a lifetime.

They were waiting for the commissary, who arrived by car. The chauffeur opened the car door, and the wife stepped out, red-gold hair, snakeskin stiletto heels, slender ankles in shimmering black silk. They walked down into the cellar. The woman saw the coat, and Mrs. Brücker saw the woman's face. What might she have said: Wonderful, marvelous? She turned this way and that before the mirror, took a few steps, turned again so that the hem of the coat swirled out. "I believe she was once a model," said blind Mrs. Brücker. Suddenly the cellar was alight, radiant in fact. And filled with a fruity perfume, heavy and sweet, a fragrance as from another world. The husband, the commissary, looked at his wife. He, too, was radiant. Everyone was satisfied. The moment of barter, preceded by so many other barter transactions, had arrived. Her business could begin.

"Nice," said the commissary. And seeing a vase of fireweed blossoms on the table, he added, so I'm told: "Where flowers are put on the table amid such ruins, the country will soon bloom again. They really are a capable lot, the Germans," and apparently he shook my father's hand, the victor honoring the vanquished. Unfortunately, though—my father translated the commissary's words—unfortunately he had no vegetable oil. Mrs. Brücker froze. "You could've knocked me over with a feather." She put her hand on the squirrel coat. But he had something else, he said. He could offer five sides of bacon or a one-kilogram tin of curry powder. Mrs. Brücker stood there, her hand on the squirrel coat, thinking it over. Five sides of bacon was a good offer, of course, easy to barter for something else, easy also to use and offer at the food stand, but curry: That made her think of Bremer, of the night they had lain side by side on the mattress island and he had told her the story of how curry helps people suffering from depression, of how in his dream he had to laugh so hard at himself that his ribs hurt, and that after all she was getting this whole lot in exchange for his lucky charm, the silver equestrian badge, and so, in defiance of all economic sense and reason, she said: "I'll take the curry."

"For God's sake, I thought, what am I going to do with the stuff?" But by that time she was already sitting in the small army truck being driven home. And the driver, an Englishman with sandy hair and a sandy moustache who kept waving his stubby, nailless index finger in front of his nose, talked away at her. She didn't understand a word, not a single word. She nodded and thought about that crazy barter. How could I? she thought. While still in the truck she tried to open the can so she could taste the spice. The Tommy took a screwdriver out of the storage compartment. After prying open the lid of the can, she dipped her finger in the powder and licked it. Horrible. The flavor, a bitter hodgepodge—no, red-hot as if fishhooks were being raked across her tongue. Ghastly. "My God, I thought, I must have been crazy. Did I take leave of my senses? What am I to do with the stuff? Who'll take it off my hands?" It could only be bartered at a loss. Apart from the whiskey, the cigarettes, and the ketchup, she had bartered the equestrian badge for something not fit to eat. If only she'd kept the squirrel coat.

The Tommy helped her carry the cases of ketchup upstairs. From the third floor, where the light always went out, they groped their way. Then it happened: She of all people, Lena Brücker, who had gone up and down those stairs hundreds, thousands of times, who unhesitatingly, blindly, could continue on because she knew every step, every rough spot on the stairs, stumbled. She stumbled because she was thinking of the curry powder, of the can she was carrying on top of the carton of ketchup, although actually she was thinking of Bremer, thinking of how they had walked up these stairs more than two years ago, thinking of how they had lived up there for twenty-seven days, in perfect harmony, until that quarrel, until he had hit the door handle until his hand bled, until she had seen those terrible photographs, until he had left, wearing her husband's suit, simply disappeared, as only men can disappear. And she went hot with shame each time she thought about what he must have thought of her when at the end of those four weeks he had walked through the city as if through another world. She had always hoped he would turn up one day so she could explain everything. But she had never heard from him again. And then—she had stumbled on the dark staircase. Splat. Three bottles of ketchup were broken. She switched on the light at the top and unlocked the door. A red mess. And in the mess there was also the curry powder from the can she had opened in the truck so she could lick the powder off one finger. And she sat down on the stairs and burst into tears. She couldn't explain to the Tommy, who tried to comfort her, that it wasn't the three broken ketchup bottles, nor the spilled curry powder, nor that she disliked the taste of the stuff, nor that she believed she had made the worst imaginable barter of her life, and certainly not that she had been thinking of Bremer, who had up and left, or of her husband, whom she had kicked out, and that meanwhile her hair had gray streaks in it but would soon be quite gray, that everything in the last few years had somehow passed her by, almost unnoticed—except, of course, for the days with Bremer. The Tommy offered her a cigarette, so, when the light went out, they were sitting side by side on the stairs, sitting in the dark and smoking, without speaking.

Then, after finishing her cigarette, already the

second that day, she stubbed it out on the metal tread, walked up the few remaining stairs, and switched on the light. The Tommy carried the other things up for her, raised his hand, and said: "Good luck. Bye-bye," then walked down. She waited by the switch so the light wouldn't go off until she heard the front door close downstairs.

Then she lifted up the carton with the intact bottles and the three broken ones and carried them into the kitchen. Fortunately the bottles weren't in such small splinters that she could only have tipped the red-brown mess into the garbage. She fished the broken glass out of the ketchup. But the ketchup, now mixed with the curry powder, was ruined. She brought over the garbage can and was about to throw away the mess when, lost in thought, she licked her fingers—licked again, wide awake, and again: it tasted, had a taste that made her laugh, pungent, but not only pungent, there was also something fruity-moist pungent about it. She laughed at the mishap, at this lucky break, laughed at the lovely squirrel coat now being worn by the commissary's beautiful wife of the red-gold hair, was glad she had kept the man on here in her apartment, laughed out loud at how she had kicked out her husband and slammed the door behind him.

She put a frying pan on the gas ring and poured in the curry and ketchup she had salvaged.

Now, slowly, the kitchen was filled with an aroma—an aroma from the *Thousand and One Nights*. She tried a little of the warm, red-brown mess, tasted it, it tasted, yes, what did it taste of? There was a tingling on her tongue, her palate seemed to expand, yes, that was what's so difficult to describe, with bitter or sweet and certainly not with pungent, no, the palate seemed to arch, you became aware of it and of the tongue, an amazement, something that concentrated on itself, on the act of tasting. Ali Baba and the Forty Thieves, The Rose of Stamboul, Paradise!

She spent the evening experimenting, taking little samples from the mess off the floor, adding a little peppermint and a pinch of wild marjoram, neither of which tasted that good, tried a few drops of vanilla, which was good, with some black pepper given her by Holzinger, a little of the rest of the nutmeg she had scrounged for Bremer's mashed potatoes, and some aniseed. She tasted the red-brown concoction: That was the perfect balance! There were no words for it. And because she hadn't had anything to eat since breakfast, she sliced one of the skinless veal sausages into the pan and cooked it up with the curry mixture. And what would otherwise have tasted merely dull and bland was fruity-moist with an exotic, indescribable flavor. She sat down and ate the very first curried sausage with zest. At the same time she wrote down the recipe on a scrap of paper torn from an old magazine, making a note of the spices listed on the can, also of her own additions: ketchup, nutmeg, aniseed, black pepper, and fresh mustard seed (actually intended for warm compresses).

Next morning, a wet, cold, gray December day, the very air was gray, the first customers turned up at Mrs. Brücker's newly opened food stand: first came the hookers from the cheap brothel on Brahmsstrasse, hollow-eyed, worn out, done for. But imagine the kind of things they must have had to submit to. Nothing existed that didn't exist. They had a lousy stale taste in their mouths, and now they wanted something hot, even if it was outrageously expensive, a cup of real coffee and a frank or a fried sausage, whatever was available. But today there were neither franks nor fried sausages, today there were only wrinkled sausages. Looked like a joke. These were then actually chopped up and covered with a horrible red sauce, or rather, a red-brown mush. "Disgusting," said Moni, but then, after the first mouthful, the taste made her sit up. "Man alive!" said Moni. The gray air lightened. The morning chill became bearable. She was getting really warm, the heavy silence turned loud. "Yes," said Lisa, "it sings, it really does!" Lisa, who had been working in Hamburg for the last three months, went on: "That's just what a person needs, it's really hot stuff!"

Thus began the triumphal march of the curried sausage, starting from Grossneumarkt, then to a stand on the Reeperbahn, then to St. Georg, then and only then with Lisa to Berlin, where Lisa opened a stand on Kant-Strasse, then to Kiel, Cologne, Münster, and Frankfurt, but strangely enough stopping at the River Main, where *weisswurst* held on to its territory. Instead, curried sausage found its way to Finland, Denmark, and even Norway. The southern countries, on the other hand, turned out to be resistant. What is essential, as Mrs. Brücker rightly says, is for a westerly wind to blow through the trees and the bushes. Its origin is linked to the gray of the north—and its opposite in terms of flavor is red-brown. The upper classes of society also proved to be resistant; none of the Perrier/boutique crowd eat it because you have to do so standing up, between sunshine and showers, alongside a pensioner, a young flipped-out girl, a vagrant reeking of piss who tells you his life story, a King Lear, so there you stand, with that taste on your tongue, listening to an incredible story about the times that gave birth to curried sausage: ruins and new beginnings, sweetly pungent anarchy.

And one day Bremer also appeared at the stand.

He had come from Braunschweig to Hamburg, gone to Brüderstrasse, looked up at the window, and said to himself how nice it would be if he were still living up there and didn't have to travel as a salesman for windowpanes and putty. He had wondered whether he should go up and ring the bell. But instead he walked on, through the streets he didn't know though he had lived in the area for almost four weeks. He came to Grossneumarkt, saw the food stand, wanted something to eat, and then he saw her. He didn't recognize her at first. She was wearing a head scarf and a white smock. Black-market dealers crowded around the stand over which, as a protection from the rain, a camouflage army tarp was spread—the tarp he had been given, in April 1945, for sleeping on the Lüneburg Heath and as a camouflage from advancing enemy tanks, the tarp under which he had walked with her through the rain.

"One of those sliced sausages, please."

She recognized Bremer immediately. She had to turn around to take a deep breath, to hide her trembling hands as she cut up the sausage. He had slimmed down again, and he was actually wearing her husband's suit. It was the most durable, the best English cloth. He was wearing a hat, a genuine Borsalino that he had acquired by barter. Business was good. At that time putty was in demand since so many windowpanes had been broken. He hadn't changed one bit, only the hat was drawn well down over his eyes. "Coffee?" she asked in his direction. "Genuine coffee?" He looked like a successful black-marketer. "Whatever," he said, thinking she must recognize him by his voice. "So what's it to be?" she asked. "Genuine coffee is two cigarettes or thirty marks." He still couldn't taste anything, and it was all the same to him whether he drank genuine coffee or acorn coffee, but then he did say: "Real coffee." "Plus curried sausage," she said, "comes to five cigarettes." The prices were steep. But he nodded. She had placed her curry mixture in the pan, an exotic aroma, then added the ketchup and finally the browned sausage slices. She pushed the slices toward him on a small tin plate. With a toothpick he speared a slice of sausage and dipped it again into that dark-red sauce. And now, suddenly, he could taste something: a paradise opened up on his tongue. While he ate the sausage, he watched her serving, smilingly, quickly, how she talked to the customers, joked with them, laughed. Once she glanced across at him, briefly, with no surprise or astonishment, saw a smiling face— beaming in fact—as if he had just made a wonderful discovery, had recognized her. For a moment she hesitated, was about to say Hello, but just then another customer asked for some acorn coffee. Her

hands were no longer trembling. He carefully
mopped up the dark-red sauce with some bread, then
handed back the tin plate. Walked on a bit and looked
across again to the stand. She lifted her arm to push
back a loose strand of hair from her forehead. A
strand of gray hair that hardly showed among the
blond, in fact enhanced it, made it look lighter. Then
she picked up the ladle and poured that red sauce
over the sausage slices. He could see—and that's how
I remember her too—that she repeated this movement day after day; it was a graceful, brief movement,
light and effortless.

She held up the half-finished sweater: the sun
was now a bright yellow ball in the blue of the sky.
"Well, what do you say now?"

"Simply beautiful."

"I'll have to see about the cloud, whether I can
still manage it."

She looked beyond me and moved her lips,
counting stitches again.

She looked frail, but with a great inner toughness,
yes, strength. I meant to ask her whether she had ever
run into Bremer again, but since I had another ap-
pointment that evening and it was already quite late, I
thought, There'll be time for that, I can ask her

another time. But then there wasn't another time after all.

The next day I went back to Munich, and soon after that for a few months to New York.

When I returned to Hamburg after six months or so and telephoned the old-age home, the doorman told me: "Mrs. Brücker? She died." "When was that?" "A good two months ago. Are you a relative?" "No."

"What was the name? Just a moment," said the voice. "There's a parcel waiting for you here. You can come and pick it up, but be sure to bring some identification."

That afternoon I drove to the old-age home and was sent by the doorman to the director's office. A heavily made-up young woman pushed a small parcel across the desk to me, didn't want to see my identification, saying that with every decease something gets left behind, "we're glad when anyone at all comes to pick the stuff up. Hugo? No, he's left. Going to university now." But she couldn't tell me where.

I took the parcel, wrapped in red paper with a design of little Santa Clauses, and left. It was March, and the pitiless urge for copulation was driving the blackbirds in the bushes to jump on each other. I walked to the car, drove a little way, stopped, undid the bow of the fine gold cord, and unwrapped the paper that had been so neatly folded, probably by Hugo. It contained a sweater. I lifted it out, and a scrap of paper fell to the floor. On the sweater a landscape, two pale-brown hills, between them a valley, on the right-hand hill the fir tree, dark green, above was the sky, a bright yellow sun, and then there was also a little white cloud drifting somewhat fuzzily into the blue. No, I realized at once that I would never wear this sweater, but I could give it to my young daughter, who likes curried sausage.

I picked up the scrap of yellowed paper, obviously torn from a magazine: on it were listed, in Mrs. Brücker's bold round handwriting, the ingredients for curried sausage. On the back of the paper is part of a crossword puzzle, filled out in capitals that I assume to be Bremer's. Some of the letters don't add up to words, others can be guessed at, as, for example, the missing "sit" for "Til." But there are still five complete words: capriole, ginger, rose, calypso, squirrel, and, slightly torn—even though nobody will believe me—novella.